AFFAIR TO DIE FOR

WENDY OWENS

For more information about the author and her books, visit her website https://shop.wendyowensbooks.com/

Editors: Jenny Sims and Karen Lawson

Formatted with Vellum

For my friend, Nic. May you soon find yourself on a beautiful beach with a good friend. Cheers.

PART ONE

JASON MCALLISTER

ONE

JASON

I sit at my mahogany desk, the glow of dual computer screens casting a sterile light across the meticulously organized surface. The world outside this room may spin in chaotic unpredictability, but I am sovereign here, within these four walls. My wife, my business partner, and our so-called friends will never understand this. I was born with the natural ability to wield power in this world. That knowledge has given me the authority to create success after success. The pending acquisition of the tech company I have spent the past four years building will be no different. It will happen and be a success because I am at the helm.

A soft click breaks my concentration. With her gait that sways between defiance and submission, Victoria interrupts my domain's sanctity. She leans against the doorframe, arms folded, her eyes scanning the room like she's searching for something more than just my attention. This casual invasion of my space irks me.

"Jason," she begins, her voice threaded with a feigned nonchalance. "Would you mind checking the alarm system? There's been something odd about it lately."

Odd, she says. The word hangs between us, dripping with unspoken implications. My company designed the alarm system, which uses AI to alert the homeowner of any unusual activity. I eye her carefully, wondering if she's purposely trying to irritate me.

"I doubt that," I answer dismissively.

"I'm serious." Her voice ticks up. "I got three notifications yesterday while I was at my hair appointment, and all of them were from regular deliverymen. I thought it was supposed to only alert us when it was an abnormal activity."

"Perhaps it's the AI trying to tell you that the amount of online shopping you do is abnormal," I reply gruffly.

I watch as Victoria's expression shifts from annoyance to hurt. A flicker of vulnerability crosses her face before she quickly masks it with a practiced smile. Moments like these make me question the tightrope balance we dance upon in our marriage. She knows exactly which buttons to push, just as I do.

With a sigh, I push back from my desk and rise to my feet, towering over her with all the commanding presence I can muster. "Can it wait?" I ask, my tone even.

"Please, Jason," she insists. "I'm sure it'll only take a moment."

I let out a sigh, one designed to show both my annoyance at the interruption and my magnanimity in granting her request. "I promise I'll take a look at it, okay? Just not right now; I have a meeting in the city."

She crosses her arms and widens her stance, looking back at me defiantly. "Why don't you ever listen to me?"

My jaw tightens in response to her question. "I'm out here trying to make the money you love to spend, so I'm sorry if I can't give you my undivided attention, darling."

"Fuck you," she growls, her nostrils flaring.

"Fuck me?" I chuckle. "That's lovely. I'm so glad you appreciate everything I do for you."

"Everything you do for me?" She gasps as she tosses her hands up in the air before they settle on her hips. "I'm trying to tell you that your piece of shit AI is busted in the nicest way possible so that you don't humiliate yourself at these fucking meetings."

As Victoria's words linger between us, a tense silence settles in the room. I can see the anger simmering beneath her carefully controlled façade, the fire in her eyes challenging me. For a moment, I consider putting her in her place, reminding her of her position in this house and my life. But then, a different thought crosses my mind. What if she's right? What if something is wrong with the AI system I designed?

Suppressing a surge of defensiveness, I take a deep breath. "Fine. I'll take a look at it, okay?"

Victoria's surprise is evident on her face for a split

second before she schools her features into a neutral mask. "Thank you," she replies, and I can tell she wasn't expecting my answer.

I step forward, and her frame softens as I press my lips to her forehead. She hesitates for a moment before meeting my gaze directly. "I have to get to this meeting, but I promise I'll get to it as soon as possible." I glance down at my watch, and even though I technically don't have to leave for another thirty minutes, I know a little distance from my wife would help clear my head. "I have to go."

Her eyes widen as she peers up at me. "When will you be back?"

"It will probably go late." She sighs in response to my words. "Victoria, you know how these things go." The tension between us crackles like electricity. Victoria's eyes flash with unshed tears. My frustration bubbles beneath the surface, threatening to spill over at any moment. She knew what she was getting into when she married me, yet she was always full of complaints about my schedule.

Victoria's shoulders slump slightly, the fight draining out of her as quickly as it had come. She gives me a curt nod before turning on her heel and stalking out of the room, her footsteps echoing down the hallway.

As the sound of her heels fades away, I sigh and rub a hand over my face. What is happening to us? The tension between Victoria and me seems to grow thicker by the day. Part of me wants to blame her for being so demanding and ungrateful for all I've provided for her. But another part of me, a small voice I've tried to ignore, whispers that maybe I've also played a role in this unraveling marriage.

The confrontation with Victoria has left a sour taste in my mouth. The last thing I need is her putting me off my game before a big meeting. As confident as I am in my AI, she has created a small nugget of doubt in my mind. I'll check the security footage from my phone before my meeting. Any concerns that there may be a shred of truth to her words will be put to rest.

I step into the hallway, and the familiar scent of vanilla lingers in the air. It is a stark reminder of Victoria's presence, even in her absence. Shaking off Victoria's unwelcome thoughts, I gather my belongings and make my way to the front door. I hesitate, considering the option to yell out a goodbye, but then think better of it. After all, she was the one who chose to storm off like a petulant child.

I close the door behind me; the sun is about to disappear over the horizon. Slipping into the driver's seat of my sleek black sports car, a sense of relief washes over me as I prepare to slip away from the suburban prison.

I pull out of the driveway, my mind still reeling from my encounter with Victoria. Her accusations and anger all feel like they're suffocating me. With a deep breath, a new resolve settles within me. I will prove her wrong about the AI system. I will show her that she was mistaken in doubting me.

Arriving at the restaurant where my meeting is set

to take place, I park and pull out my phone. Connecting into Haven, the AI interface I created, I pull up the video footage for my home and flip through the alerts. A knot forms in my stomach when I see three alerts, just as Victoria had said. I play the clips, and sure enough, they are all package deliveries with nothing out of the ordinary occurring during the drops.

This is not how Haven is supposed to behave. A package delivery does not represent a threat. If the delivery person were to look through the window or something, I could see why Haven would send the alert, but I rewatched the clips several times, and there was nothing.

"Fuck," I hiss as I realize my wife was right. I'm about to walk into a meeting to pitch the acquisition of Haven, and everything I have been touting she is capable of is complete and utter bullshit. This can't be right. She was working perfectly. We've tested Haven repeatedly. If she can't identify something as trivial as a package delivery, what if she misses an actual threat? Jesus Christ, I am so fucked.

I pull up the source code for Haven and start to look for anything out of the ordinary. Nothing. Everything is as it should be. Frantically flipping through the screens on my phone, I return to the logs from our home. Something had to cause Haven to start behaving that way. I'm sure of it. I click on the summary report from my home, and that's when I see it. There's a gap. Someone else may have missed it entirely, but not me. I type in a command, asking Haven to explain the mysterious gap in the logs.

She replies the gap resulted from footage being deleted from the security feed. It doesn't make sense. Victoria knows better than to delete anything from Haven. That data is what helps her identify potential abnormalities. Perhaps it was an accident. I ask Haven how many clips have been deleted. Seven. The answer causes my face to flush hot in anger. Seven is not an accident.

My heart races as a new realization sets in—I've been betrayed. My wife, Victoria, has been manipulating the AI system I designed. Why? To what end? Is she trying to make it seem faulty in order to plant seeds of doubt in my mind? It doesn't make sense. She'll benefit from the acquisition of Haven just as much as the rest of us.

I sit there in my car, frozen in shock for what feels like an eternity. My buzzing phone breaks through the heavy silence and pulls me back to reality. It's a text message from Victoria. Hope your meeting goes well. Sorry if I upset you.

A bitter laugh escapes my lips as I read her message. "You fucking bitch," I mutter.

I turn my attention back to Haven. I dig through the lines of code in an attempt to restore the deleted footage. I hold my breath as Haven processes my request. Every passing second feels like an eternity as I wait to see if the recovery will be successful.

Finally, a notification pings on my phone, signaling

that the footage has been restored. Of course, she wasn't smart enough to actually delete the footage. With trembling hands, I open the video feed and watch the missing clips from the security camera play out before me. My heart pounds in my chest as I see the truth unfold.

There she is, Victoria, standing at the front door with a young man in the image. His face is familiar, but I can't place where I know him from. They speak in hushed tones, their body language tense. As I observe the exchange, a wave of nausea washes over me when I watch him step into our home. I flip to the following clip. It's more of the same. Clip after clip is this young man entering my home. He looks in his early twenties. Jesus, where the fuck do I know him from?

Betrayal courses through me like a bitter poison as I realize the extent of her deception. I never actually see them touch or kiss in any of the clips. Maybe there's a chance that it's not what it looks like, but then why delete the footage? How long has this been going on? How could she do this to me? Questions without answers echo in my mind as anger simmers beneath the surface.

I click the replay button. The footage begins again, their body language too comfortable, too familiar. I zoom in on Victoria's face, scrutinizing every flicker of her eyes and the curve of her lips into a smile that isn't meant for me.

Each viewing carves a deeper notch of suspicion into me. Her laughter reaches through the silent digital playback, a soundless ghost taunting me. How she tilts her head toward him is intimate, conspiratorial.

I am Jason McAllister, master of my domain. Yet here I am, dissecting pixels to make sense of my wife's potential deceit. How dare she? Doesn't she know who I am and what I'm capable of?

Their interaction plays again, and a cold realization settles in. This is not just about infidelity. Victoria is purposely making a fool of me. She must have known she created a glitch in Haven when she deleted the footage. Fuck. That fucking bitch actually has the confidence to think I won't be able to recover these clips.

I zoom in on the young man's face and take a screenshot. These two are about to learn precisely how ruthless I can be.

I play the scene one more time. "Got you," I whisper, freezing the frame where Victoria's gaze locks onto the camera lens for a fleeting second. Is that a glint of defiance I see? Or guilt? It doesn't matter. What matters is that she has forgotten the cardinal rule of our life together—I am the center, the sun that she orbits.

I sit back in the driver's seat of my car, my mind racing with a flurry of emotions. As I stare at the frozen frame, a plan begins to form. I will not be made a fool of in my own home by my own wife, no less. I will not allow her to manipulate me or play games behind my back.

First thing tomorrow, I'll call Marshall. I've used him in the past to look into possible investors and even competitors. Having a little dirt on those you're doing business with never hurts. I can trust in his discretion when it comes to this matter. He'll be able to help me place the familiar face of the young man spending so much time with my pretty little wife. He'll also be able to confirm my suspicions of Victoria's betrayal.

My wrist vibrates as my watch notifies me it's time for my meeting. With my concerns about Haven's integrity evaporating, I close my eyes and take a deep breath, centering myself. I step out of the car, a newfound resolve hardening within me.

I straighten my suit jacket. Inside, I will play the part of the successful entrepreneur. As long as it benefits me, I will continue with the façade I have constructed as the doting husband, praising his beautiful wife. But make no mistake, Victoria has declared war with her betrayal.

TWO

JASON

The elevator dings its arrival on the floor of Haven's offices. I step out with the usual brisk confidence that marks my morning. But today, a fog of unease clings to me like a second skin. Purposely, I came home after I knew Victoria would be asleep, and I left before she awoke. The last thing I want right now is to look into her dishonest eyes. It was hard enough to share a bed with her last night after I knew she had been lying to me.

As I walk by the rows of cubicles toward my glass-walled sanctum, my gaze snags on a mop of tousled brown hair, and my stomach tightens. The young man is hunched over his desk. My pulse quickens as a jolt of recognition hits me. It's been less than twelve hours since I stared at the grainy doorbell cam footage, but there's no mistaking that profile. It's him—Victoria's secret visitor, caught on camera. Fuck, I knew he looked familiar. He's a goddamn employee here.

"Good morning, Mr. McAllister," the young man greets when he realizes I have caught him in my sights.

Shit, what is his fucking name? Now that I've seen him, I know I've spoken to him at least half a dozen times. My jaw clenches as I try to maintain a façade of calm. "Good morning, uh . . ." I stall, my mind racing to recall his name.

"Lucas." He fills in the blank for me, offering a polite smile.

Right, Lucas. In return, I force a tight-lipped smile, my thoughts consumed by questions swirling in my mind. How long has he been seeing Victoria behind my back? How did they even meet? Do they think they're clever enough to outsmart me? The nerve of them both.

As Lucas nervously shuffles some papers on his desk, a surge of anger bubbles inside me. But I can't let it show. Not here, not now. I need to play this strategically. I continue, greeting my assistant who informs me my coffee awaits me inside. I close my door before collapsing into my desk chair.

My mind is a storm of questions. I may have mistaken the interaction I witnessed on the camera. After all, this Lucas kid works here. It wouldn't be impossible that he was running errands for Victoria. Maybe she met him one day when she stopped in the office, and this is as simple as him picking up our dry cleaning. I tense. The body language I witnessed between them didn't seem harmless. I can't simply disregard this as nothing. If I let it go and there is, in fact, something between them, it would be humiliating.

I reach for the burner phone tucked in the back of my desk drawer. I occasionally have to make certain calls that I would prefer there not to be a record of, and the one I am about to make is one of those. I flip through the list of previously dialed numbers until I spy the familiar one I need and press call.

"Marshall," the familiar gruff voice answers after just two rings.

"Hey, Marshall, Jason McAllister here. I have another job for you." I lean back in my leather chair, eyes fixed on the ant-like people bustling on the streets below.

"Hit me," Marshall replies, the sound of shuffling papers filtering through the line.

"This one will require the utmost discretion," I begin, my voice lowering as if someone could overhear me in my sealed office. Marshall's experience and professionalism keep me coming back to him for these delicate situations.

"You know that's how I handle all my cases," he replies, and I sense a tinge of annoyance.

"Of course you do. That's why you're my go-to guy," I reassure him. "I need you to tail someone for me. Keep an eye on her every move and report back to me."

"Okay, no problem," he answers without hesitation. "Who are we talking about?"

"My wife," I say and wait for his reaction.

"Anything in particular I'm looking for?"

"Everything," I stress, the word cutting through the

air, leaving no room for ambiguity. "Every single thing she does and every person she has contact with. I want photographs, a timeline . . . Document it all."

"Understood," Marshall responds, the faint pen click indicating he's taking notes. "I'll get on it."

This is why I go to him when I have these needs. No questions, just action. I wish everyone in my life was as reliable as Marshall. Relief washes over me like a cool wave as I thank him and hang up. Did Victoria really think she could deceive me? The thought of her betrayal sends a surge of anger through me. No one—no one—makes a fool out of Jason McAllister.

My fingers drum against my desk. Victoria's image flits across my mind's eye, her brittle smile false and ungrateful. After all, I've provided her with a life most women would be envious of, and she dares to betray me? She better hope it's not what it looks like. That fucking kid out there is more than ten years younger than I am. If she has done what I think she has, I can't begin to think of how I will punish her. When I'm done, she'll have nothing. And when she begs for my forgiveness, I'll make sure she knows this was all her doing.

All I have ever asked from her was complete loyalty and obedience, and in return, I give her a life of luxury. The terms are so simple, yet they seem to elude her. The thought of betrayal, like acid, churns in my stomach. A part of me, a dark sliver of vindictive satisfaction, relishes the idea of catching her in the act. To watch her crumble under the weight of evidence and see the realization dawn on her that she destroyed everything.

Punishment is only just if it serves as both retribution and a reminder. And oh, I will remind Victoria of the vows she took. She's not just a wife; she's a reflection of me, and any tarnish on her is a blemish on my image and my reputation.

My thoughts are interrupted by a gentle knock on my door. I look up as my assistant pokes her head inside. "Jason? Do you have a second?"

"Of course, Jenny, come in," I reply with a smile as she steps inside and closes the door behind her. I watch her as she approaches my desk, her outfit perfectly hugging her ample curves. I lick my lips, suddenly hungry for a taste.

"I wanted to thank you for the necklace. It's beautiful." Her voice is like a lifeline.

For a moment, I fumble mentally, the jewelry a distant thought compared to my wife's treachery currently consuming me. But then, the mask slips back into place—the smooth smile and effortless charm. "I'm glad you liked it."

She puts her hands on the corner of my desk and leans forward so that her cleavage is pushed out, the gift in question dangling in front of those magnificent breasts. Her eyes are scanning my face with a perceptiveness that irks me. I don't need her concern. "Is everything okay?"

The weight of her gaze is heavy on me.

"Just a lot on my mind," I reply, keeping my tone light. "You know how it is."

She straightens up, adjusting her blouse subtly

before speaking again. "Okay, if you say so." She hesitates before she continues. "But I want you to know you can tell me anything."

I sigh. "Things at home aren't going great," I confess.

"Oh no, really?" she asks softly, her eyes growing wide. "What's wrong?"

I want to tell someone what is happening, about how Victoria has ruined everything we had, and confirm I am not wrong for feeling the way I do about her betrayal. "It's just . . . Victoria," I say, letting the name hang in the air like a poisonous cloud. "She's been acting strange lately. Distant. I'm starting to think —maybe—there might be someone else."

Jenny's hand flies to her mouth in shock. Her eyes are filled with a mixture of disbelief and concern. "Oh, Jason, I'm so sorry."

I nod, my façade of vulnerability firmly in place. "I don't know what to do. I thought I gave her everything she needed, but now . . ." I allow the unspoken accusation to linger between us.

Jenny gently places a hand on mine, her touch electric against my skin. "I'm so sorry you're going through this right now."

I meet her gaze, letting a flicker of gratitude pass through my eyes before masking it with a look of resignation. "Thank you. Your support means more to me than you know."

"Of course," she answers with a nod.

I drink in her words and let them wash over me like a balm to the sting of betrayal. It's validation.

Clearing my throat, I shift the subject. "Is Declan in his office?"

She nods. "I saw him come in earlier."

"Good, I need to get back to work." The command is gentle but firm, and she understands, retreating with an obedient nod.

"Oh. Right, of course you do. Let me know if there's anything else I can do." As the door closes behind her, her promise lingers in the air, rich with implication.

I watch her go, the sway of her hips a temptation I can hardly resist. But now is not the time for distractions. I need to focus on the task at hand. I have an acquisition I'm working to close on and a cheating wife I have to destroy. First on the agenda is a visit with my business partner, Declan, and a discussion about his laughable performance at last night's business dinner. I can't continue carrying everyone in my life. It's time for the people around me to start showing up when I need them, including him.

———

THREE

JASON

Victoria stands before the full-length mirror, the soft glow of the evening light casting a halo around her. She's an ethereal vision, her slender fingers delicately adjusting the straps of her emerald gown, the fabric hugging her curves with precision and grace. The dress makes her eyes pop—a color you don't forget easily, like the first shoots of spring grass.

"Jason, how do I look?" Her voice is a sweet melody that makes me cringe inside when I think about her lies.

I step out of the closet, fixing my cuff links, catching my reflection briefly—crisp tuxedo lines, every piece in its ordained place. "You look beautiful," I say, and it's no lie. But then I attempt to slice at her with my words, as sharp as a razor's edge. "But where do you think you're going?"

Confusion flickers across her face. She turns toward me, the movement fluid like a willow swaying in a gentle breeze. "The same place you are," she replies, a touch of amusement in her tone. "The mayor's dinner."

Her confusion is a delicate thread, one I'm eager to pull. Her presence at the event is a benefit she has lost the privilege of. But she doesn't know that yet.

I shrug off her confusion with a practiced ease, the way I might dismiss an underling's trivial mistake at the office. "Oh," I say as if the thought has only just occurred to me, "I guess you don't remember me telling you."

"Telling me what?" she asks, her eyes fixed on me through the mirror's reflection.

"They were only able to secure one table this year for Haven. That means no spouses, unfortunately." I watch her face for the hurt. My words are a lie—punishment for her unseen transgressions.

She shakes her head. "No, you never told me that."

I scoff. "I'm sure I did."

"Jason, please. I've been looking forward to this event for months," she protests, her voice tinged with disbelief. Her hand pauses midair, fingers hovering over the delicate fabric of her dress. "We go to the mayor's ball every year. I don't understand. It doesn't make sense."

I lean against the mahogany dresser, arms folded, and watch Victoria's reflection in the mirror. She is a study of elegance, marred by the crease between her brows and the way her lips press into a thin line.

"Really, Victoria, I'm sure I mentioned it," I say with a lightness. "But honestly—you've been so wrapped up lately . . . in your own affairs, I'm not shocked you forgot." There's a subtle emphasis on the word affairs.

She turns to face me, her expression crumpling for a split second before she regains composure. "My own affairs?" Her voice climbs. "What is that supposed to mean?"

I shrug, feigning nonchalance. "I don't know what you mean," I counter, watching her closely. Her hands clench at her sides, knuckles whitening.

"Why are you doing this?" she demands, stepping closer. Her gaze searches mine. "Why are you acting this way?"

Her question hangs between us, charged and heavy.

"I'm not acting in any way," I answer coolly. "I couldn't get a second table this year, so you won't be attending tonight. That's the end of it."

Victoria's eyes widen in shock as the weight of my words sinks in. Her hands tremble slightly at her sides, her chest rising and falling with rapid breaths. I watch as a myriad of emotions flicker across her face like shadows dancing in the moonlight—confusion, hurt, and a spark of defiance.

"I don't understand," she finally manages to say, her voice barely above a whisper. "You know you never told me. I can't believe you're really going to leave me here."

"Sorry, Victoria," I say with false sympathy dripping from every word. "I'm almost positive I told you, but either way, there's nothing I can do about it. There simply isn't a seat for you."

A flicker of something dangerous flashes in her eyes before she quickly turns her features into a mask of resignation. She squares her shoulders, lifting her chin in defiance.

"Well then," she begins, the words sharp and pointed like daggers aimed at me. "Enjoy your precious event, Jason."

I tilt my head, feigning concern. A smirk threatens to surface. "You always do this. When things don't go your way, you become irrational. Sometimes you can be so selfish."

She blinks at me, her eyes aflame with indignation, and I can see the gears turning. "Selfish? Irrational?" The words explode from her. She steps toward me, her elegant heels clicking against the wooden floors as she moves.

"Jason, you're being completely unreasonable!" Her voice grows louder. "Can't you see this from my perspective for once?" There's a raw edge to her plea, a crack in the façade I'm all too eager to exploit.

I back away slowly. "I'm not going to do this with you."

"Do what with me?" she demands, matching me step for step.

"I won't stand here and be spoken to like this when we both know how it will end."

"What the hell are you talking about?" she shouts.

"There, that's exactly what I'm talking about." I throw my words at her. "You always have to escalate things to an unhealthy level."

She follows. "You're the one twisting everything! You're the one being selfish!"

Her accusations hang in the air. With a scoff, I turn on my heel, heading for the front door. When my hand grasps the door handle, I turn toward her to deliver my final blow. "I'm selfish, huh? Who goes to work every day so we can afford things like that stunning gown? Or how about the diamond necklace you have on? I'm such a selfish asshole for giving you everything you ever want."

The air in the foyer crackles with electricity, and my exit is halted by the softening of Victoria's voice. I pivot slightly—coolly regarding her downcast eyes and the way her hands nervously play with the fabric of that expensive dress I bought her.

"I'm sorry," she murmurs, the fight draining from her voice. "I-I just got upset when you told me I couldn't go, and—you're right. I was being selfish. Can you forgive me?"

Her plea, laced with desperation, is music to my ears. I let the silence stretch for a moment longer than necessary, watching as she squirms under its weight.

I sigh before I finally offer her the words she desperately searches for. "Of course I can. I always forgive you, Victoria. That's what someone does when they love someone."

"Thank you, Jason," she whispers, relief evident as her posture relaxes ever so slightly.

"Let's forget all about it," I say with calculated

grace. "Enjoy your evening here. I'm sure I'll be back late, though, so don't wait up."

And with those parting words, I press my lips to her forehead and step out into the night. Victoria will spend the evening alone, questioning herself and her actions—as she should.

FOUR

JASON

My fingers tapping the keyboard halt as Jenny's voice crackles through the intercom. "Mr. McAllister, there's a Marshall Scott here to see you." A surge of anticipation courses through me, and I straighten up in my leather chair. This is it—the moment I've been waiting for.

"Send him in," I reply, trying to sound unbothered, but I can't help the edge of eagerness in my voice.

The glass door to my office swings open, and the man of the hour steps inside. Marshall Scott's very name sounds like someone who gets things done, no questions asked. He carries himself with a certain gravitas, a fixer down to his core. His eyes, sharp and assessing, miss nothing.

He's wearing a nondescript gray suit that blends into the background. A crisp white shirt peeks under his blazer, the top button undone. My attention immediately homes in on the folder he has clutched in his hands. I must resist the urge to cross the room and rip it from his possession.

He closes the door behind him with a soft click, a sound that marks the boundary between the outside world and the revelations about to unfold within these walls. I press the button under my desk, which closes the privacy shades of my glass fortress. The last thing I need is prying eyes, wondering who this man is and why he's here.

I motion for Marshall to take the seat across from my desk, trying to mask my impatience. "I have to admit, I didn't expect to hear from you so soon," I say, my eyes flicking to the folder in his hand. "It's only been a week since we spoke."

Marshall takes the seat and offers a nod, his expression unreadable. "This isn't like the normal tasks you require of me. Corporate surveillance requires much more finesse. Your wife, on the other hand—well, she made my job very easy," he replies, and my stomach tightens at the weight behind his words. He clears his throat and gives a slight, almost indistinguishable chuckle that sets me on edge before he continues. "She's been a very busy lady." His voice is even, but I catch the implication.

"Is that right?" I ask matter-of-factly.

He nods. "I assumed you'd want to know sooner rather than later." There's a hint of caution there, a prelude to bad news.

"Cut the pleasantries, Marshall," I snap, more

sharply than intended. My hands clench into fists on the desk. "Just tell me what you've found."

He meets my gaze squarely, no flinching. "You're the boss—but just a warning, you might not like what's inside this folder."

"Goddammit, just fucking show me already," I demand, my tone brooking no argument. He has clearly forgotten who he's talking to, as pity is the last thing anyone should offer me. Pity is for people who are not in control of their own destiny, and that has never and will never be me.

"Of course, you're the boss," he says as he leans forward and slides the file across my desk. I slam a hand onto the top of it to stop it from sliding completely off the surface. Opening the folder, I spread the contents out in front of me. They're glossy, full-color betrayals—photographs that punch the air from my lungs. Victoria and Lucas, her laughter caught in still life, his hand possessive on her waist.

My face flushes red, a silent roar of anger echoing in my skull, yet I somehow keep my voice controlled and steady.

"I assume this was what you expected me to find?" Marshall asks with certainty in his voice.

I ignore the question as I continue studying the images. I notice multiple outfit changes between them. "You've only been following her for a week. How many times did they meet?" I ask, my fingers grazing an image of them kissing—a public display of her infidelity.

"Three confirmed encounters," he answers in a low rumble.

"That fucking bitch. Out in public—" I hiss, barely containing the venom in my words. "Jesus Christ, they're standing out on the sidewalk where anyone can see them." The thought alone ignites a fresh wave of fury. How it reflects on me, her carelessness and complete disregard for the humiliation it would cause me. Making her miss the mayor's dinner is nothing compared to the punishment she deserves.

"Yeah, she didn't seem concerned anyone would recognize them. Honestly, she looked right at me at one point, and I was worried she may have made me, but then she went right back to what they were doing," Marshall says with no judgment in his tone.

I sit back, forcing my composure to return, though the redness in my cheeks remains. I scan every photograph and every document, committing them to memory. Each image is another nail in the coffin of the carefully constructed life I've built. I can't decide if Victoria only has a total lack of regard for me or if she's too stupid to think of how much damage this could do to my reputation. Either way, it's unforgivable.

The silence in the room thickens as it wraps a chokehold around me. My mind races. The pictures lie scattered on the desk, proof of Victoria's indiscretions. I can see the potential headlines on the society pages and the whispered gossip at the country club. My reputation in this town is everything. The last thing an investor wants is to put his money in a company where the CEO's wife doesn't respect him.

"Fucking bitch," I growl under my breath.

Marshall shifts in his seat, the leather creaking under his weight. "When Mrs. McAllister wasn't with the young man in these photographs, she kept to her routine—meeting friends, shopping, going to the gym. Nothing out of the ordinary."

"Of course, she did because Victoria's entire existence is nothing out of the ordinary. Everything interesting about her is because of me," I state before collecting the images and sliding them back into the folder. I take a deep breath, releasing it slowly as I regain a semblance of my composure. "Thank you, Marshall. Your work has been . . . thorough."

Marshall nods, his expression unreadable. "Do you want me to continue to keep an eye on her?" His voice maintains its professionalism.

I shake my head. "No, that won't be necessary." The words taste like ash in my mouth. "I believe I have everything I need. I think it goes without saying, but discretion is key in this matter."

"Absolutely, sir. You have my word," Marshall reassures me as he stands.

"Make sure it stays that way," I reply, my gaze locking onto his.

"Of course," he says. "I will delete the images from my laptop now that I have handed them over to you. You will have the only copy of them." He moves toward the door and then pauses briefly. "I'll send my invoice this afternoon."

I offer a tight-lipped smile before shoving the file into my top drawer and locking it with the key in my pants pocket. "Thank you. You can see yourself out."

I'm alone, the silence deafening after the storm of revelations. I stand and walk to the large window that overlooks the bustling street below, then begin to pace. My thoughts whirl, dark and treacherous. I can't let her deed go unpunished. The desire to confront Victoria burns within me, a fire I struggle to contain. But no, not yet. Such impulsivity is beneath me. If I act rashly on this matter, it could blow up in my face. I need to think this out carefully.

My gaze lands on the framed degree on the wall, the accolades, the family portrait where we all smile, perfect and unblemished. They're a testament to what I've created, my kingdom. Yet behind Victoria's smile in that photograph is a secret now laid bare by grainy images in a PI's folder.

In my world, you don't give your opponent the satisfaction of knowing they've gotten to you. You don't show weakness. It's not just about teaching Victoria a lesson; it's about sending a clear message that loyalty to me isn't optional. You are either with me or against me, and she has made it clear where she stands.

A smirk tugs at the corner of my mouth as I consider the endless possibilities. A public revelation? Too messy, and while it would hurt her, it would also reflect poorly on me. Quietly cutting off her funds? Tempting but not quite enough. No, whatever I do must be calculated, a move so subtle yet devastating she won't realize what's happening. A blindside of sorts.

The problem is I'm so blinded by my anger I'm having trouble seeing which strategy is best for me to move forward with. I need another set of eyes and ears on the problem, and when it comes to this, only one person comes to mind. The one person who would stand to lose as much as I would if my reputation were tarnished. My business partner, Declan. We have a bidding war in the early stages for Haven. If this were to suddenly get out, potential buyers may question my leadership. After all, who could respect a man whose own wife steps out on him?

I compose myself, taking long, calming breaths as I walk away from the window and toward the liquor cabinet. Pouring myself a glass of aged scotch, I sip it stealthily, the burn in my throat reminiscent of the fire raging within me.

As much as it pains me to admit it, I know I need an outside perspective to help me navigate this situation. He could never be the leader that I am, but he has his usefulness. I dial his number. Declan picks up on the second ring, his deep voice filling the room.

"Jason, what is it? I was just heading out for a round of golf," he utters with a soft chuckle.

"Of course you were," I say dismissively. Declan's work ethic pales compared to mine, but he comes with many influential connections.

"Is that judgment I hear?"

"Are you still in the office?" I ask, ignoring his sniping comment.

"Yes—" His voice cracks with hesitation. "But I have to leave in twenty to make my tee time."

"I'll be right there," I state, hanging up before he can protest.

I pour myself another drink and swig the amber contents down before slamming the glass onto my desk. I may not be certain about how to proceed with Victoria, but one thing is certain. A plan is forming, and once I chat with Declan, nothing in the world will stop me from making sure my beautiful wife fully understands the consequences of her treachery.

FIVE

JASON

I stride down the hall toward Declan's office. His door is ajar. The walls of his workspace are adorned with generic prints, the kind you'd find on the walls of any budget-friendly hotel. Declan's obliviousness to the power of appearances never ceases to amaze me. It's like he doesn't realize that every detail crafts the narrative of one's existence.

"Declan," I call out as I knock on the frame of his open door.

He looks up from his cluttered desk, his gaze landing on me. There he sits, decked out in slacks and a pink polo shirt that screams casual Friday rather than Thursday hustle. As I shut the door behind me, his eyes follow my movements, a flicker of curiosity lighting up his otherwise indifferent expression.

"Ready for the golf course, I see," I say, narrowing my eyes at him while taking a seat across from his desk.

"I told you, twenty minutes, and I'm out of here.

There's nothing like a nice round of golf to clear the cobwebs and help get you back into the mainframe of being productive. You should try it sometime," Declan replies.

"I don't have cobwebs that need clearing," I remind him. "I wake up in productive mode."

"Ah, yes." He chuckles. "Sometimes I forget who I'm talking to. Jason McAllister, the king of efficiency. So what brings you here today, Your Majesty?" He leans back in his chair, all too casual for the bomb I'm about to drop on him.

My heart pounds as I prepare to reveal the dark thoughts swirling in my mind. "It's about Victoria." I watch Declan's face closely for any sign of shock. Still, there's just a flicker of interest.

"Is that a new shirt?" I ask, dodging his question.

He glances down at the pastel pink draped across his chest before answering, "No, I think I've worn it into the office before."

"Jesus, man, I was kidding," I reveal. "You look like a sixty-five-year-old retiree down in Florida instead of a powerful executive in his thirties about to embark on one of the biggest acquisitions this town has ever seen. It's fascinating how you haven't snagged yourself the perfect woman yet. Did you ever think maybe it's the wardrobe?"

Declan chuckles, a mischievous glint in his eyes as he leans forward slightly, resting his elbows on the cluttered desk. "Ah, but you see, Jason, not all of us are looking for the perfect woman. Some of us are too preoccupied with sealing deals and making millions to bother with such trivial matters." The smirk on his face doesn't quite reach his eyes,

I resist the urge to roll my eyes. "We both know that's not true, Declan. You are about as far from a workaholic as one gets."

"Hey, not all work is done in the boardroom," he chimes defensively. "It may look like I'm out there slacking off, but those relationships I build on the back nine are where we are getting a lot of the interest in our bidding war."

He's not wrong.

"Fine, fine," I concede with a wave of my hand. "Fair point."

"I'm assuming you didn't want to come in here to discuss my wardrobe choices," Declan adds, eyeing me. "Care to tell me who pissed in your Wheaties this morning?"

"Sorry," I say, the word tasting like vinegar on my tongue. "It's been a rough morning."

"Rough in what way?" Declan leans forward, all pretense of casual disinterest slipping as he senses the undercurrents of my discontent.

I take a deep breath, steeling myself for what comes next. "Victoria . . . she's been having an affair," I admit, the words heavy with betrayal and anger.

Declan's expression remains carefully neutral, though I catch a flicker of something else in his eyes before it disappears. "An affair? Are you sure about this, Jason? Victoria has never seemed the type," he asks in a deceptively calm tone.

"Oh, and you are suddenly the expert on cheating wives?" I snap back.

Declan raises his hands in a calming gesture, his eyes never leaving mine. "No need to get defensive. I'm just trying to wrap my head around the situation."

I let out a frustrated sigh, running a hand through my hair. "I have evidence, Declan. Photographs showing she's been seeing someone behind my back."

"Jesus," he grunts in disbelief. "Do you know who with?"

I scoff as I can hardly believe the words about to come out of my mouth. "You won't believe it when I tell you." I shake my head. "You know that punk kid, Lucas?"

Declan's chuckle grates on me. "Lucas? Are you serious?"

"That's funny? Why's that? Because the kid is ten years younger than me?"

Declan shrugs. "Well, try fifteen years, but no. I can't believe the cojones on that kid to fuck your wife after what we had him do. I mean, Jesus, you'd think the kid wouldn't want to piss you of all people off, knowing how far you would go to get what you want."

I frown, confusion knitting my brows together. "What are you talking about?"

"Really? You don't know who that kid is?" Declan's amusement fades into incredulity.

"Declan, do I look like I want to play a game of

fucking twenty questions? Just spit it out," I snap, patience worn thin.

"Lucas was the intern over at Manhattan AI Solutions. He's the one we gave that nice fat bonus to and a promise of a full-time position down the road in exchange for him bringing us—certain information."

"That's him?" I ask, leaning back as I process the fact that this was the kid we had hired to be our corporate spy. We needed someone insignificant to pull off the task. Someone nobody would notice.

"Beverly tells me the kid is also known to charm the ladies." Beverly is Declan's busybody assistant, and her opinion isn't one I would ever seek out. "Maybe cut Victoria some slack. Lucas is a hustler—like us." Declan's words attempt to soften the blow, but they fall flat.

"No offense, but both of you are nothing like me." I narrow my eyes at him.

"Well, no one is like you, Jason," Declan concedes, a wry smile playing on his lips.

I lean forward, my voice low and filled with resolve. "I can't let this affair slide, Declan. It's not only a matter of pride or betrayal. If word gets out about Victoria's infidelity, it could affect the way investors see the CEO of this company. This could affect you just as much as it does me."

"So talk to Victoria. Tell her what you found out. I'm guessing this was a cry for attention." His suggestion causes my spine to go rigid.

"A cry for attention?" I repeat the words. "Are you

fucking with me right now? It's not like she spent too much on her credit card; she fucking cheated on me, man."

"Jason, aren't you being a tad dramatic?" he teases, leaning back with his irritating smugness. "Given your own . . . let's call them 'extracurricular activities.' How many is it now since you tied the knot with Victoria?"

His words are barbed, and I feel the sting. My jaw clenches. "My activities, as you call them, are not even comparable to her betrayal. Those were just sex. What she did . . . no, it's so much worse than that. I provide for her and give her everything she could want, and she publicly flaunts her boy toy around town. And not just any boy. She has to pick someone who works for my company. This is personal."

Declan watches me, the amusement fading from his face as his gaze hardens into something more calculating. He leans forward, elbows on the desk, fingers tented together. "That might be, Jason, but there's nothing you can do about it."

"What's that supposed to mean?"

"Remember the divorce clause in the company bylaws?"

I snap at him, irritation bleeding into my tone. "I don't need a reminder, Declan. I helped write those damn bylaws." My hand slams onto the desk, a punctuation mark to my frustration. The rule was meant to protect us in case one of the board members found himself in a situation where his wife was entitled to half his shares in the case of a divorce. Rather than getting tied up in litigation, fifty percent of the executive's shares would be sold to the remaining board members. It kept everything in-house and, at the time, felt like the safest option. I never imagined they would ever apply to me.

Declan continues, his voice steady. "If you lose even half of your shares, you realize it could tank the pending acquisition." His eyes bore into mine, ensuring I grasped the full weight of his words. "Imagine if Tom or Ryan get their hands on the shares up for grabs after your divorce. They've already made it quite clear they are against the sale."

The unspoken threat hangs between us as clear as day. The office walls seem to close in.

A chill runs down my spine as Declan's words echo in the confines of my skull. My vision blurs momentarily. When it clears, I'm staring at the man across from me with newfound clarity. Divorce isn't a personal failure; it's a professional suicide vest strapped to my chest.

"Shit," I mutter under my breath.

"Jason?" Declan prompts.

I look up, meeting his gaze. "You're right," I say, my voice steady despite the turmoil. "Divorce will cost me everything."

"So you're going to try to work things out with her, then?" Declan attempts to clarify.

I nod slowly, a plan fermenting in the darkest recesses of my mind. It's vile, despicable even, but desperation has a way of stripping away morality, leaving only the primal need to survive and conquer. "It would seem that's my only option, wouldn't it?"

He's watching me. "You've always been a pragmatist."

Every breath I draw in is a gasp of clarity, which only comes when you're teetering on the edge of an abyss. Victoria, my dear, deceitful Victoria, has become a liability too great to shoulder. To lose control, to have my empire crumble because of her infidelity . . . it's unthinkable.

I murmur, my voice a low thrum of determination, "It would be terribly unfortunate if something were to happen to Victoria." I watch him closely. "We live in such precarious times, don't we?"

Declan doesn't blink. Instead, he lets a slow, almost imperceptible smile tug at the corner of his lips before it vanishes as quickly as it appeared. He knows exactly what I'm suggesting without a single explicit word passing between us.

"Jason," he says, his eyes devoid of any emotion that could tie him to this conversation later, "I don't want to hear anything else about it." His chair pushes back, and he straightens his pink polo shirt, a stark contrast to the dark thoughts swirling between us.

"There's nothing else to say on the matter," I assure him.

He clears his throat before casually adding, "Remember, I have a tee time to make."

"Of course," I reply, my mind already churning.

"Good luck on the green," I say, but the words are empty and hollow.

"Thanks," Declan says with a nonchalance that belies the gravity of our exchange. I follow him toward the door and exit with him before heading back to my office to further contemplate my next steps.

I don't feel an ounce of remorse or guilt for what has to be done because Victoria sealed her fate by her own betrayal. She is the maker of her destiny and has forced my hand.

SIX

JASON

The sizzle of eggs hitting the hot pan doesn't drown out the clinking of her wedding ring against the skillet handle. Victoria moves through our kitchen with the same grace and routine she's shown since we moved into this suburban mausoleum of a home. My gaze is locked on her, not out of admiration but rather an ever-deepening well of disgust that churns in my stomach. She hums some tuneless melody, oblivious to the storm brewing across the room.

"Jason?" Her voice cuts through the silence, a faux cheeriness clinging to each syllable. "What are your plans for today?"

I press my fingertips into the arms of the chair, feeling the leather yield beneath the pressure. It takes effort to peel my eyes away from the sharp knife she wields so carelessly as she chops strawberries—a metaphor if there ever was one. "What they are every day—Work," I grunt without looking at her.

She giggles softly, and I'm amazed she can behave like everything is normal around me. It's not simply that I've discovered she's a liar; it's also the fact that I have realized she is a damn good one. There isn't a single blemish in her façade.

"No, silly, I know that you are going to work. I just meant, is there anything special happening at the office?" The persistent chirp of her words used to endear her to me, but now it's a grating peck at my patience.

"Meetings," I respond, curt and clipped.

She turns, flashing a smile meant to thaw the frost between us, but it's too late. The unyielding cold within me has already settled deep in my bones. "Well, I hope they go well."

My fingers twitch, a visceral response to suppress the bile rising in my throat. "They always do." I force the corner of my mouth up into a semblance of a smile, knowing full well it doesn't reach my eyes. Eyes that no longer see the woman I married, only the lies and betrayal that have taken her place.

The clink of porcelain against granite punctuates the end of Victoria's breakfast preparation. She swivels toward me, her face alight with an idea that seems to inject some animation into her graceful movements. "What do you say we do something together tonight? Just the two of us?"

I catch a whiff of her perfume as it drifts across the room. Victoria had been giving me the cold shoulder ever since I took away the mayor's dinner, and I must admit her sudden shift in attitude puzzles me. Perhaps she's feeling guilty for her betrayal. It would make sense, considering how she has disrespected me after I have given her the life she always desired. I muster the energy to craft a smile, though it feels like stretching a canvas over a frame that's too large. "What brought this on?"

"What do you mean?" She plays coy. "You've been so busy lately, but I was thinking it would be nice for us to spend some quality time together." Her eyes connect with mine, and she lifts her brows at me while pursing her lips, and suddenly, I understand exactly what she's saying. Victoria and I have always had a pretty healthy sex life, with us usually being intimate at least five times a week. That has changed since I saw the footage of her and Lucas. Since then, I haven't been able to touch her, and it's clear she has taken notice.

If she thinks she's going to outplay me, she is sorely mistaken. I watch as Victoria's mask slips for just a moment, a flicker of uncertainty crossing her features before being replaced by that same serene smile. I can see the gears turning in her mind, calculating and assessing, but she underestimates me.

"Sure, sounds good," I reply smoothly, knowing that playing along is the only way to keep up the charade for now. As she moves closer, her hand inching toward mine with a practiced familiarity that now feels like a mockery, I resist the urge to pull away. This is just one more act in her elaborate performance.

"Great! It's a date," she chirps, and I nod.

She chatters on as I scarf down the breakfast she prepared for us, wanting to be as far from her presence as possible. When I finish, I shove my plate forward and flip through the calendar on my phone. Minutes tick by, and I can feel her energy as she flits around the kitchen, cleaning up. Her expression is one of someone who believes they have a future worth looking forward to. The irony tightens my jaw.

Eventually, she finishes tidying and grabs the gym bag from the hallway before approaching me. "Well, I better get going. I signed up for the early morning cycling class today because the afternoon one was full," she explained, describing information I could literally not care any less about. I used to think Victoria maintained her tight body for me, but now all I can think about is that it's for men fifteen years younger than me.

She leans in for a goodbye kiss, and I hesitate, the war within clear on my face if she'd only look close enough. But she doesn't. With a reluctant tilt of my head, I let our cheeks brush, a peck so fleeting it might as well be a whisper.

"See you tonight," she says, all smiles and ignorance as she turns for the door.

"See you," I echo back, the words hollow. The house is silent as the door closes behind her.

Suddenly, my phone buzzes an invasive vibration that jolts me back to the present. It's Declan. The text glaring up from the screen reminds me of normalcy. Don't forget our 10 a.m. meeting.

My thumb hovers over the keyboard, rage

simmering as I ponder his words. With terse precision, I tap out my response, making sure Declan understands his concern is unwarranted. I've never forgotten a meeting in my life.

Seconds later, another message from him, a veiled reference to the whispers of trouble brewing in my household. Just thought you might be distracted with everything at home.

A bitter laugh escapes me. Distracted? If only he knew the clarity with which I see the world now. I punch back a reply. Not needed. Perhaps focus on your own work instead.

Declan's response comes almost instantaneously, a brief Got it that does little to quell the tension settling in my bones. I shove my phone into the pockets of my tailored pants and grab my blazer off the back of the dining room chair, sliding it on. It's time to head to the office, and I welcome the distraction.

Grabbing my bag, I make my way out to my car and slide into the leather driver's seat. Last night, my mind was restless, churning over the future I was shackled to. My conversation with Declan brought something significant to the foreground. A divorce would likely torpedo the pending acquisition as it would trigger the sale of half my shares to existing board members. I clearly don't have the funds available right now to purchase them, which would mean they would more than likely get snatched up by other board members with a different vision for the company. Unthinkable.

The other option would be to wait it out and not get

divorced until after the acquisition goes through. No, that would be even worse. Then she'd be entitled to half of everything I built with my own blood, sweat, and tears. And that cannot happen.

My grip tightens on the steering wheel. Initially, the thought was simple: Victoria's demise masked as a random act of violence. But as the idea took root, it grew thorns. It's not enough. Lucas needed to pay too. The audacity of this kid to think he can just waltz into my marriage and make a mockery of me? It's a debt that demands retribution.

But it's not so simple to make the pair pay in the way I had initially thought. How could I orchestrate their end so it appears random?

That's when it hits me with undeniable clarity. I need to weave a narrative where Lucas becomes the architect of his and Victoria's destruction. It has to be a situation that is believable without question. The kid is young and obviously impulsive. Perhaps he will be the jealous lover, unhinged by Victoria's attempt to reconcile our marriage. The story will spin itself: a tragic ending for two lovers caught in the throes of passion turned sour. In the aftermath, sympathy will fall on me, the grieving husband, wronged yet dignified.

My image will remain untarnished as my sweet Victoria had made the decision that she made the biggest mistake of her life when she cheated on me. It's so perfect I can barely contain my excitement. I need to map out the details, each step with surgical precision.

By the time I'm through with Lucas and Victoria, it will be a closed case. A crime of passion—so cliché and so effective. No one will question why the young lover snapped when faced with rejection. People love a story they've heard before because it requires no effort to believe.

The office comes into view. Moments later, I pull into the parking lot and kill the engine. A smile creeps across my face at the simplicity of it all. Victoria will receive no sympathy, as people will say she deserved what happened to her for being unfaithful to me in the first place. Lucas will be perceived as the destroyer of homes, just as he is. I'm the only one who will come out of the situation with an image better than when I went into it.

I step out of the car and make my way into the building, my mind already formulating the next steps of my intricate plan.

As I pass by my employees, exchanging pleasantries and feigning interest in their mundane lives, I can't help but feel a surge of power coursing through me. This power, this control over the narrative, emboldens me. I navigate through the office with newfound confidence, my mind consumed by thoughts of the scenes I will orchestrate.

Every detail must be meticulously planned, and every action must be calculated to ensure the desired outcome. I map out hypothetical scenarios, anticipating every possible deviation from the script. This isn't only about revenge; it's about crafting a masterpiece of deception that will secure my future while sealing their fates.

SEVEN

JASON

I gaze at the reflection staring back at me from the rearview mirror, practicing a smile. It's all about perception. If Victoria believes our marriage is stronger than ever, she'll be blinded by love or at least the illusion of it. She won't suspect a thing. Bonus points if she spills to her friends about the doting husband she has. If she paints a picture of her perfect marriage, no one would ever believe I could be behind the fate that will befall my wife.

The weight of my phone in my hand reminds me of the role I have to play. My thumb hovers over the screen before I tap out a message.

Where are you, love?

Her response comes quickly. Just got back from the gym, hopping in the shower. Why?

I can almost hear the water running, the image of steam and soap bubbles. But I push them aside. This isn't about desire; it's about strategy. I type back with feigned warmth. Just missing you, that's all.

Her following text pops up. Are you feeling okay? Did someone steal your phone? She adds a laughter emoji as if that somehow softens her nasty attempt at humor.

Never better, I assure her. Just wanted to remind you how much I adore you.

The charade gnaws at me, a relentless itch beneath my skin. Each syrupy word I dispense is like swallowing glass, yet I bear it with a grin. It's the price of admission to the grand finale—my revenge.

I park in our driveway, slip out of the driver's seat, and head inside, where I can hear the water running upstairs. I tread lightly up the stairs, each step bringing me closer to the role I must play to perfection. The bathroom door is ajar, steam billowing out.

I linger at the threshold, watching the steam rise and twist into nothingness. But for now, I'm here, and so is she—oblivious, vulnerable, and so very trusting. She's already inside the shower.

I strip away my clothes with mechanical efficiency. As I step into the steamy veil of the shower, Victoria releases a startled gasp. Her eyes widen. For a moment, I see her as she once was before her betrayal tainted everything.

"Jason!" she exclaims in surprise.

"Miss me?" I murmur.

She recovers quickly, a smile spreading across her lips. I allow myself to be drawn in. My hands roam her body with feigned adoration, each touch calculated. I plant kisses along her neck, my lips trailing to her collarbone, eliciting soft moans from her that belie the revulsion churning within me.

A stray thought pops into my mind when she exposes her bare neck to me of how easy it would be to wrap my hands around it and squeeze until the last bit of life leaves her body. I force the thought far away, unwilling to let this whore bait me into making a mistake that will land a fatal needle in my arm.

"Jason, this is . . ." she breathes out, her words lost in the rush of water and the intensity of my ministrations.

"Shh," I whisper against her skin, silencing any further speech.

I lift her effortlessly, her back against the cool tiles. My mouth finds hers. I explore the terrain of her hips and thighs. She wraps her legs around me in response. The intimacy feels like a sharp blade in my chest, but I push through. I'm on a mission to pleasure her and make her believe.

My fingers delve into her, seeking out the places that will drive her wild. Her gasps fill the space between us. I watch her face contort in pleasure.

"Jason," she whispers my name like a prayer.

"Let go, Vic," I coax, knowing that her release is the crescendo to this act, the proof I need that I've played my part well.

And she does, her body tensing, then shuddering under my touch. I continue to move with precision, drawing out her pleasure. Eventually, she falls limp in my arms, spent from the force of her climax. As she clings to me, all I can think about is why I am doing this. For the greater good, for the endgame—that sweet, inevitable downfall that awaits her.

With her still quivering from the aftershocks, I'm determined to finish what I started. I can't come with her looking at me, so I flip her over and grab her hips as I drive myself deep into her. She cries out, and there is a tinge of pain mixed with her pleasure. I grow harder when I hear the vulnerability. Excitement builds in me, and I slam harder into her. With each thrust, I bring her closer to her end. I'm not just fucking her but punishing her. She tries to wriggle away from the intensity, but I hold her tight. I sink deeper into her, and her muscles clench around me.

"Jason!" she gasps. "Please . . ."

Her pleading thrills me. She's begging for relief, and I'm not giving an inch. The power is exhilarating.

Her cries grow louder, more desperate.

A sudden change in her expression makes my heart pound in my chest: dread. Could she sense what I'm doing? Understand this isn't about passion or intimacy? That this is a power play? My heart races so fast that it's challenging to focus on anything apart from the pounding in my ears.

Slowing down, I pull out almost entirely but leave just a hint of me inside her, enough to feel the tension coiling between us. "Are you okay?" I ask, my voice a velvet rasp.

Her eyes are wide, and her breathing is shallow. She nods, but the lie is evident on her face. "Jason, I—"

I thrust into her again, and she whimpers in response. I lean in and press my lips to her shoulder. It's a tender promise that everything will be alright, even as I grip her hips and thrust once more. The rhythm is slower now, deliberate, designed to draw out her response.

Each stroke takes us closer to the edge. Each gasp from her lips fuels my desire. Her body clenches around me.

"Jason . . ." she breathes again, the word a mere whisper now. And then she comes undone beneath me, her body jerking and pulsing around me until she's crying out in a mixture of pain and release.

I seal the performance with the final mark of my own satisfaction. We stand there, entwined under the relentless stream of water as if we could wash away the lies that bind us. The act is complete, and the curtain falls.

"Jason," she breathes, and I almost falter at the name —not because it's mine, but because of its tainted echo in my memory.

"Victoria," I whisper, the name leaving a bitter taste. But she hears only tenderness and sees only love.

The hot water cascades over us, rinsing away the remnants of our frenzied union. I reach for the shower gel, and my movements are mechanical.

"Here, let me," Victoria says with a smile. She takes

the bottle from my hands. She's oblivious to the rage behind my placid exterior.

I focus on maintaining the mask as she lathers the soap over my skin. I stand there motionless, letting her ministrations continue as I calculate each breath, each reaction, ensuring they all read as love.

We finish rinsing off in silence, which speaks volumes only to me. It's a quiet that hums with the unsaid, with the weight of what's to come. Stepping out of the shower, I grab a towel and wrap it around my waist, watching as she does the same. Droplets of water race down her body. For a moment, I can almost appreciate its aesthetic beauty.

"What's gotten into you, Jason?" she asks.

She's looking at me with those eyes. The ones that once pulled me in but now feel like they're mocking me.

"I'm sorry I've been so distracted with work lately." My hand reaches out, tucking a wet strand of hair behind her ear. It's a gesture that I know she finds endearing. "But I love you, Vic. I promise I'll be around more as soon as I close this deal."

There's a sparkle in her eye, a glint of happiness that I did not expect, momentarily piercing through the armor of my resentment. This is the woman I married, the face of innocence that once made my heart surge with genuine affection. But that was before betrayal soured its sweet taste to bile.

"I appreciate you saying that. I can't wait to spend more time with you," she says. Her lips peck my cheek, leaving a warm imprint that feels like a brand.

"Neither can I," I lie smoothly.

She leans in and embraces me in a brief hug, burying her head into my chest. She whispers her gratitude, which sends a shiver down my spine. "I'm such a lucky woman," Victoria breathes out.

My arm wraps around her waist. "You deserve everything I give you." My carefully crafted phrase would be revealing if she knew I had discovered her betrayal.

But she doesn't know that. She can't see past the veneer of the doting husband. And why would she? After all, I've played the part to perfection.

EIGHT
JASON

Another week bleeds into oblivion, each day indistinguishable from the last because every moment is spent counting down to the time I will be vindicated. Seven days have passed—seven days since I made the decision to bring an end to two people who have injured me as no one else ever has.

I have been playing my part as the loving husband when I am with Victoria with fervor. As much as it pains me, our intimate encounters now pepper our nights with increased frequency. Each touch, each whispered word, it's all choreographed. She knows nothing of my true intentions. The plan I have that will rob her of her final breath.

She sighs and murmurs sweet nothings, and I return them—not out of desire but necessity. I can't risk her suspecting that I know what she's been up to with her young lover when we are apart. It's imperative to keep the mask secure and maintain the façade of a loving husband.

It's a grotesque mimicry of love, but it serves its purpose. Every calculated caress, every feigned moment of ecstasy, they're all required as part of the plan. Victoria remains none the wiser.

I trace the curve of Victoria's spine, my fingertips deliberate in their path, a feigned tenderness. She arches, unwittingly compliant to my touch. The room is dim, our shadows mingling on the walls.

"Jason," she whispers, breathless, unaware that she inches closer to her end with each utterance of my name.

"Hmm?" I murmur back.

"Can you stay with me today?" she pleads, mistaking my distant gaze for emotional depth.

"Babe, I wish I could, but you know I leave for the conference tomorrow. I have to take care of a lot of things at the office before I head out." I lie smoothly. I hold her close, a lover and executioner in one, and savor the irony that we have never been further apart in these moments of closeness.

She pushes out her bottom lip, pouting to elicit sympathy from me. I force myself to feign concern.

"I know you have to go. Lately, I just feel like we have been so connected," she confesses.

"I agree. I know it sucks when I have to go out of town, but I'm sure you'll find something to busy yourself with," I reply, the photographs of her and her lover flashing through my thoughts.

As Victoria's head rests against my chest, her breathing steadies into a peaceful rhythm. In the stillness of the early morning, I let myself feel the sadness I have forced myself to keep at bay. A part of me still loves Victoria, and perhaps that's what hurts the most. Her lack of care for how her betrayal would impact me makes it unforgivable.

The conference will be my alibi, meticulously planned and flawlessly executed.

"I know; I'm just having a pity party for myself," she says, sighing heavily.

I envision the scene unfolding later this evening when I bring her a gift for which she will be so thankful —flowers and a bottle of her favorite champagne—but it is all part of my seamlessly scripted plan. She will be giddy in her excitement when she sees the treasures I've brought her.

But I know. I know she won't be able to resist the urge to share a glass of her favorite bubbly drink with her young lover. The soft clink of crystal against crystal as Victoria raises her glass, unaware of the danger that lurks within. The taste of deceit will be masked by the sweetness of her favorite champagne, tainted with a dose of Rohypnol . . . I've done my research. The effects take around twenty minutes, but then I will have up to twelve hours with the pair to set the scene.

My grip tightens imperceptibly around her, a silent vow to see this through to its bitter end. When her breathing steadies and I feel her relax as she drifts off into slumber, I resist the urge to brush away the strands of hair from her face.

The dawn breaks in hues of crimson and gold, and with calculated precision, I rise from the bed. I leave Victoria as she falls deeper into her post-passion rest. Making my way to the shower to prepare for the day ahead, I catch a glimpse of my reflection in the bathroom mirror. I can see the anger, hurt, and betrayal simmering just beneath the surface. I steel myself, knowing I will set everything right soon enough.

Once dressed in my sharp suit and tie, I make my way downstairs and step out into the crisp morning air. As I head toward the office, I pull out my burner phone and dial the number of the man I need to help me complete my plan.

"Mr. McAllister, I didn't expect to hear from you again so soon." Marshall's voice comes through the line.

"I need your assistance with something," I say, hoping my request can be met quickly.

"Of course, whatever you need."

What I'm about to ask him for will prove how much trust I have in the man. While a part of me is concerned it could be misplaced, I feel confident in my decision to seek his help. I've researched and understand the dosage required to ensure neither Victoria nor Lucas will wake up mid-scene. The plan is simple: use a syringe to lace the champagne. As she sips, growing drowsy, I'll paint the picture of an intimate night turned tragic.

"What I'm about to ask of you can never be traced

back to me," I state, making sure he understands that our conversation never happened.

Marshall's silence on the other end of the line stretches, the weight of my words sinking in. I can almost hear the cogs turning in his mind as he processes the gravity of my request. But to his credit, he responds with unwavering determination. "I understand, Mr. McAllister. You can count on me to handle it discreetly."

Relief washes over me. "Can you obtain a bottle of Rohypnol for me?"

There isn't a moment of hesitation before he responds, "No problem."

"I need it today," I add.

"I'll text you a time and location," he replies without a hint of doubt.

As I end the call, a sense of satisfaction settles over me. This is going to happen, and nobody will even consider I could have been the one who orchestrated the entire scene. I reach the office. The hours pass in a blur of meetings and mundane tasks, my outward demeanor a mask of professionalism that hides the fact my thoughts are consumed with planning out the details of each second of the following day.

Marshall isn't the only person I need help from to properly execute my plan. If I rent a vehicle to drive from San Francisco to LA, there will be a record on the car's GPS. I need to borrow a vehicle to make the drive that can't possibly be traced back to me.

I reach out to an old business acquaintance,

someone I don't particularly like but who owes me a favor. Rick owes me for vouching for him with an investor. He had led an investor to believe that he had raised the initial funding for his company despite not raising a cent. My word that he could be trusted kept investors from digging too deep and asking for proof that would have resulted in him getting caught committing fraud.

Between meetings, I close myself in my office and make the call.

"Rick, I need a favor," I say firmly over the phone, my tone brooking no argument.

There's a hesitant pause on the line before Rick finally responds, "Uh, sure Jason, what do you need?"

"I'm heading into San Francisco tomorrow, and I need to borrow a car for a couple of days while I'm at a conference."

The man chuckles. "I thought your little Haven project was paying off. You all can't even afford a rental car?"

His words cause my spine to go rigid. Your little Haven project. This smug piece of shit deserved to get outed as a fake all those years ago, and I would love to tell him as much if I didn't need his help.

"It's a matter of privacy. I don't want anyone knowing my whereabouts during the conference," I state.

"Ah, okay, man. No problem. I get what you're saying. You don't want the little lady to be able to figure out you have a little love nest up here with some young hottie, huh?" Rick replies. Fuck. I so want to punch this tool right in the face.

"You could say that," I reply, just wanting the call to come to an end before I can't manage to hold my tongue.

"I got you, bro," Rick says before his laughter crackles through the phone. "You dog."

My jaw clenches as I thank him, then tell him I need him to park the car in my hotel's parking garage and leave the keys at the front desk. He doesn't argue.

As the day begins to wrap up, I receive a text from Marshall telling me where to meet him. It's perfect. I can grab the champagne and flowers on my way to the meeting, then head home. As I leave the office, I remind Declan I need him to pick me up on the way to the airport in the morning. Declan jokes that he is also so professional he doesn't need reminding. I smirk at him, wishing I could share my plan with him. Still, I can't be foolish about this, no matter how much I am confident he would marvel at my attention to detail.

I make my way to the address Marshall sent me, my mind already jumping ahead to the next steps in my plan. Entering the dimly lit parking garage at the address he texted, I found Marshall waiting exactly where he said he would be. He approaches my vehicle and climbs into the passenger seat before pulling out a small package.

"Here it is," he says, handing over the container of Rohypnol. I nod in thanks, taking it from him and slipping it into my coat pocket. No time for idle chatter; every moment is precious now.

As I'm about to leave, Marshall clears his throat, hesitating before speaking up. "Mr. McAllister, I don't want to know what you're doing. I feel like someone should ask if you're sure you want to go ahead with whatever you are planning?"

I fix him with a steely gaze. "I'm sure."

He gives me a curt nod and exits the vehicle, slamming the door closed behind him and not looking back at me.

After picking up Victoria's favorite white roses, I move to the shop's cooler, grab a bottle of her favorite champagne, and then pay with cash. Once I'm back in the car, I pull out the syringe I had hidden earlier in my glove box and use it to draw out the perfect amount of Rohypnol. Carefully, I press the needle into the cork of the champagne before depressing the plunger to deliver the dose into the fluid.

When I arrive home, the sun is setting. Victoria greets me with a warm smile, unaware of the dark thoughts swirling in my mind as I hand her the bouquet of roses. She thanks me with a kiss on the cheek.

Victoria has dinner waiting for us. When she sees the champagne, she suggests opening it for dinner. Panic tightens in my stomach at the suggestion I hadn't considered.

"Actually, you were so sad about me leaving this weekend. I bought that just for you. I thought you could have a relaxing bath one night while I'm gone and enjoy a couple of glasses," I explain.

She studies my face for a moment.

"Jason, you're full of surprises," she remarks with a smile, her eyes shining with gratitude. I can't help but feel a pang of guilt at her sincere appreciation, knowing what I have planned for her. But I push the feeling aside, reminding myself why this must be done.

After dinner, I tell Victoria I need to pack. She says she has to clean the kitchen, and I should go upstairs. Heading upstairs, I place the suitcase on the bed and unzip it.

Initially, I considered hiring someone to carry out the actual act. After all, I've never actually killed anyone before. Ultimately, I decided I couldn't risk having a loose end out there who could flip on me. A part of me also wants them to know—it has to be me who orchestrates this final act. Victoria must understand the consequences of deceiving me.

[illegible] have a relaxing bath one night while I'm gone [illegible] reading [illegible] glasses! I [illegible] for a moment.

[illegible] she remarks with a [illegible] but [illegible] feel [illegible] approach [illegible] what I have planned [illegible] inside [illegible]

[illegible] it.

[illegible] part of me [illegible] them to know [illegible] before [illegible]

NINE

JASON

The softness of Victoria's lips against mine is the last piece of tenderness she'll ever get from me. I plant the kiss gently. She is utterly convinced of the tenderness as I hold her face in my hands. Her eyes, deep pools of trust and love, don't see the storm brewing behind my own. "I'll miss you," I whisper, the lie tasting like sugar on my tongue.

"I'll miss you too, baby. Be safe," she murmurs back, her fingers grazing the lapel of my jacket as if trying to hold something already gone.

I nod, allowing a smile to play at the corners of my mouth. As I pull away, the thrill of what's to come sends a shiver down my spine that I mask with a feigned shudder of sorrow.

"I love you," I say, stepping out the door and into the crisp morning air. She presses another kiss to my lips and grazes her fingertips across the crotch of my pants.

"I love you too," she whispers. "I'm going to make sure that I welcome you home properly."

The world outside is oblivious to the game I'm playing. The car waits as a silent accomplice to my plans. Declan leans against it, his expression unreadable. Declan takes my suitcase and tosses it into the trunk as I slide into the passenger seat, the leather cool against my skin. A moment later, Declan climbs into the driver's seat. My heart pounds, not with nervousness but with anticipation.

"Well, that wasn't something I expected to see," Declan says, his voice tinged with confusion.

I chuckle. "I know you're a forever bachelor, my friend, but what you saw there is called a happily married couple."

"Since when?" He gasps as he makes his way out of our neighborhood and toward the highway.

I shake my head. "I overreacted the other day."

"So she isn't sleeping with the Lucas kid?" he asks, and just his utterance of the idea causes my cheeks to flush hot, but I can't reveal the anger rising in me.

"Honestly, I don't know."

"What do you mean you don't know? I thought you had proof," Declan argues.

I shrug. "Maybe, or perhaps it was all taken out of context."

"Did you ask her?"

I force another laugh. "I'm definitely seeing why you have never had a relationship that resulted in you getting hitched. Most women wouldn't take well to being accused of infidelity. I've decided that Victoria deserves the benefit of the doubt."

"Is that right?" he says, one eyebrow arching slightly as he glances my way.

"Absolutely," I continue, leaning back into the leather as if confidence could be drawn from its plush embrace.

"Okay, who are you, and what have you done with my business partner?"

I flash Declan a charming grin that deceives with its warmth. "You don't have to worry about your business partner, my friend. I've just had a change of heart, that's all."

He shoots me a skeptical look before returning his attention to the road. As we speed toward the airport, the trees blur past us in a green and brown haze.

"So you're really telling me that everything is good at home?" Declan asks again after a moment of silence.

I nod enthusiastically. "Better than ever. In fact, Victoria and I have been . . . reconnecting lately." The lie rolls off my tongue effortlessly, coated in honeyed words.

Declan lets out a disbelieving snort. "Reconnecting?"

I chuckle. "Oh yeah. It's like we're newlyweds again."

His eyes narrow in suspicion, but he doesn't press further. Instead, he focuses on the road ahead as if trying to make sense of the sudden change in dynamics between Victoria and me.

As we near the airport, the excitement bubbling inside me threatens to spill over. Soon, I'll be on a plane to San Francisco, far away from any suspicions and closer to my ultimate plan.

Declan pulls into the extended parking lot, and we both step out of the car and grab our suitcases from the trunk. I can feel his gaze on me, searching for any cracks in my façade. But I remain composed, my mask firmly in place.

"Excited for the conference?" Declan asks, his tone casual.

"For sure," I answer. "But I also can't wait to get back home."

He nods. I watch him for a moment, ensuring my story has taken root.

Declan turns to face me with an expression meant to be congratulatory but doesn't quite mask his doubt. "That's great, man. Sounds like you two are back on track," he offers.

I nod, trying to mirror his enthusiasm. "I can't explain it, but it's like everything's clicked into place again." My words hang between us, a delicate thread of deception I can't afford to break.

Declan chuckles a low sound that seems to carry an unspoken question. "Well, if you're happy, I'm happy for you." There's a pause, and I sense him studying me, looking for chinks in my armor. "It just seemed like things were pretty rocky for a while there, so I guess I'm having a hard time wrapping my head around it."

Rocky is an understatement, but I press on, reinforcing the narrative. "Sure, every marriage has its ups and downs. But we've worked through it. You know how it goes." I force a laugh. "Well, I guess you don't. But marriage is hard work."

I catch a look in his eye that tells me he's not entirely sold on the story. His skepticism quickens my pulse, a silent alarm that urges me to weave my tale tighter to make it bulletproof.

"Anyway," I continue as we walk toward the airport entrance. "I can't wait to get back to her after this trip. She promised she has some bedroom tricks planned that will blow my mind when I get back."

I can feel Declan's eyes on me, probing, searching for a slip—a sign that I am not the content husband and eager professional I've presented myself as. My skin tingles with the weight of his scrutiny, but I keep my steps casual, my posture relaxed.

When Victoria's body is discovered, there's always a chance the police won't simply buy the narrative I've created. I'm no fool. I know they usually suspect the husband in cases like these first. I need to know that if they interview Declan, he will confirm that Vic and I are happily married. It wouldn't bode well for me for him to even mention the conversation we shared the other day about her infidelity.

"Uh-huh," he grunts, not looking at me as the airport doors slide open.

"Look, man, I get it. I know I was pretty upset when we chatted the other day, and you have your doubts," I say, glancing at him from the corner of my eye. "But trust me, everything is fine now between Victoria and me."

Declan's lips press into a thin line as he nods slowly. "I hope you're right, man. I really do."

"I always am," I tease. "You know that."

I'm ready. Ready to play the part of the devoted husband until the final act unfolds. And when it does, no one will suspect the truth.

TEN

JASON

The cool San Francisco breeze brushes against my face as Declan and I step out of the taxi in front of the hotel. The towering façade casts a long shadow over us, starkly contrasting the bright California sun that hangs overhead. We make our way through the revolving doors, the lobby's clinking glasses and murmured conversations washing over us like a sophisticated wave.

"Jason, you up for running through the pitch before tonight?" Declan asks as he checks his watch with a brow raised in anticipation. It's clear my recent hints about his work ethic have taken root.

"Actually," I say, my voice laced with feigned exhaustion, "I'm not feeling all that great. Might just lie down for a bit."

"Oh no, it's not anything too serious, I hope?" he inquires, and I can see the concern on his face. I'm almost certain it's more likely an apprehension that he might have to carry many of the presentations we host this weekend if I am under the weather.

"Nah, Victoria and I were up before dawn, and I think it's left me pretty exhausted. Fuck." I force a laugh as I push the idea of our rekindled love home. "She's been insatiable lately."

I wasn't lying. Anytime I was around, Vic was ready for it. Still, the security footage on the home cameras revealed she was also up for it anytime Lucas was available. It shook me that she was fucking me and him on the same day. I mean, when I would have the occasion of stepping out on our marriage, I never disrespected Vic by fucking both women on the same day.

"Okey dokey," he chirps awkwardly, and I wonder if perhaps I have been trying to drive the point home a little too hard. "Well, rest up, man," he says, patting me on the back before heading toward the elevators.

We check in side by side and carry our bags to the elevator. When the doors slide open, I pretend I forgot something and tell him to head on up.

With Declan out of sight, I return to the front desk. "Hello there." I eye the attractive blonde behind the counter. She had waited on Declan, but I could feel her gaze on me the entire time.

"Can I help you, sir?" she asks, repeatedly batting her eyelashes.

"I was just here, and I forgot to ask. I had a friend who was supposed to drop off a set of car keys for me. Is there any chance some are back there with a note that they are for Jason McAllister?" I ask, my voice steady.

The receptionist offers a practiced smile as she checks the drawer to her left. She then hands over a pair of keys without missing a beat. "It looks like these were left for you."

I grasp the keys, their metal teeth digging into my palm as I clench my fist around them. Relief floods me, subtle enough not to draw attention. After a simple "thank you" to the receptionist, I head toward the elevators.

The door clicks shut behind me, a sound that ushers in the privacy I need. Once in my room, I waste no time unpacking my suitcase. I glance at the time. My plan relies on precise time management. I have no intention of going down for my crimes, meaning a solid alibi is essential. One p.m. The countdown begins.

My hands are steady as they select the attire laid out days prior—the clothes that will witness the end of my marital charade. They are dark, nondescript, and easily discarded.

The small backpack tucked inside my suitcase awaits its inspection. I unzip it slowly, peering inside to confirm the contents: a change of clothes, clean and devoid of any connection to what's about to transpire. Zip ties and duct tape lie dormant, their presence a precautionary measure. Meticulous planning has left little room for error or struggle, but one can never be too careful. Knowing I couldn't possibly smuggle a weapon into the airplane, it is hidden outside my home and awaits to be reunited with me.

With each item accounted for, I reseal the backpack.

The thrill of control, the power of orchestrating every move is intoxicating. Four and a half hours remain until the meet and greet begins for the initial evening of the conference. I will require at least six hours to drive to LA on the backroads, where no traffic camera could betray my presence. All of this has to be meticulously timed.

At 5:30 p.m., I'll make my appearance among attendees at the event. I'll do an ample amount of mingling with everyone before I display just enough discomfort to be convincing. At 6:30 p.m., I will give Declan my apologies and assurance that what ails me isn't something that a good night's rest can't cure.

His brow will furrow, and there will be a strain of concern in his voice as he checks to see if I'm okay.

"I will be after a good night's rest. I'll have my phone on Do Not Disturb to make sure I can sleep, though," I'll tell him. "But I'll catch you for breakfast."

Simple. Believable. Effective.

I draw a deep breath, allowing a moment of stillness before the storm. Then, with resolute steps, I head for the shower, letting the hot water cascade over me and wash away any lingering traces of doubt. Soon, very soon, freedom and vengeance will both be mine.

The buzz of my phone breaks the silence, a subtle intrusion that pulls me from my reverie. I pick it up, and the screen illuminates with Jenny's message. Good luck tonight. The phone buzzes again with a second message. I just wanted to let you know I've been missing you.

A pang of something akin to guilt twitches in my gut. With her doe eyes and unwavering loyalty, Jenny is a welcome distraction when the weight of my responsibilities presses in on me, but she could never be anything more. Despite that, I like having her around when the need strikes me. I have been so consumed with Victoria's situation I'm sure she feels forgotten.

"Thank you, Jenny," I reply, my thumbs tapping over the keyboard. "Lunch is on me when I return." My mind traces back to the late nights at the office, her body bent over my desk, her soft sighs—a pleasant but unnecessary complication.

I hesitate, then add, "For being the best assistant a guy could ask for." A promise of appreciation, one I'll have to honor to ensure her silence when the time comes. It's practical to keep those loyal to you feeling valued. Also, if the police ever obtain these texts, I wouldn't want them to find a motive within, and the assistant comment absolves me of a possible motive.

Moments later, hot water envelops me, a veil of steam rising around my form. I let the heat sear away any lingering tension or hesitation. Each droplet that cascades down my skin seems to cleanse me, not just of sweat and grime, but of the life I'm about to leave behind.

As water swirls down the drain, so too does the façade of the man I pretended to be. All that remains is the architect of a foolproof plan, the soon-to-be executor of a calculated end.

ELEVEN

JASON

The engine's soft purr dies as I kill the ignition and lean back into the driver's seat. A few houses down from my own, the borrowed car is hidden in the shadow of an overhanging oak. From here, I can see the dimly lit windows of my home.

Declan had bought my story of feeling ill without a blink. I was nervous someone might see me as I slipped away from the hotel, but nobody seemed to even look in my direction. Before heading to the parking garage, I retrieved my backpack and placed my cell phone in my hotel room. My hope is that the scene will be set so perfectly that there is no question of who the killer is and what the motive is, but the phone is a backup. It will serve as confirmation of an iron-clad alibi in case the police search for the GPS location of my cell phone.

I crack the window just enough to let in the coastal chill, the salt air sharp against the back of my throat. It keeps me alert and focused. The satisfaction swells within me, thick and heady, as I marvel at how flawlessly my plan has unfolded. I've always been good at the long game, but this—this is my masterpiece.

On the drive here, my secondary phone sent me an alert from Haven. The cameras I had rigged with heightened sensitivity captured a beacon of movement. My resolve strengthened, and all doubt faded when an image of Lucas stepping onto the porch appeared before me. The smug tilt of his head was visible even through the pixelated shadows. He's walked right into my web, thinking he's safe and owns what was once mine.

I watched Lucas disappear into the house, unaware of the storm bearing down on him. This man, this boy who dared to infiltrate my life, to lay claim to Victoria . . .

Pulling up the interface with Haven on my phone, I quickly disengage the video feed to our home. The last thing I want is any record of me not in the place I claimed to be tonight. With a final glance at the tranquil façade of my home, I slip out of the vehicle and move like a shadow along the edge of the street.

I'm a mere shadow under the moon's cold gaze as I stand back, surveying the house that holds everything I once cherished and now despise. Victoria, with her soft smile and lies that cut deep, could have chosen differently. She could have severed ties with Lucas when I gave her every reason to return to me and reminded her subtly of what we had.

I can taste the bile rising in my throat at the thought

of their hands entwined, the whispers shared in the bed I once laid claim to. My pulse quickens; this is more than betrayal—a festering wound that refuses to heal. The time for mulling over chances and choices is over.

My feet carry me toward the house, each step calculated and soundless. I glance around my surroundings to ensure nobody is watching. It is just before one o'clock, and our quiet little neighborhood seems to all be fast asleep. Every fiber of my being is alert, wired with the adrenaline of a predator closing in on its prey.

My fingers find the cushion on the porch chair with practiced ease, and slipping underneath, I retrieve the cold, heavy weight of the gun I hid there the previous evening. Knowing the power I hold in my hand—the power to rewrite the narrative that's been forced upon me—is a grotesque kind of comfort.

The weapon is an extension of my will. With the gun secured, I'm ready to reclaim what's been taken from me.

I'm at the front door now, more nervous than I had anticipated. My hand hovers over the brass doorknob, a slight tremor betraying the surge of emotions vying for control within me: anger, betrayal, determination. I swallow hard, thoughts swirling with visions of Victoria and Lucas intertwined in deceit just beyond this barrier.

"Focus," I whisper to myself. The cool metal feels slick against my palm sweat as I finally grasp the doorknob and hold it tight. I press the numbers into the door lock that belong to Victoria, holding my breath with each ding. When I hear the lock disengage, I turn the knob slowly, painstakingly, willing it not to make a sound.

The door yields to my touch, opening to the dimly lit foyer. I step inside, and the scent of home wraps around me. For all the pain she has caused me, that is one thing I can say that Victoria always did well. She created a welcoming home, a true oasis for me away from work. I pause and allow my eyes to adjust to the shadows.

Ahead, the staircase looms, an artery leading to the heart of memories we built together—memories now tainted with lies.

I move forward. It's hard to remember when the familiar space was filled with genuine laughter and love. Each step I take is measured and deliberate, as our past haunts me. A part of me suddenly worries if I am somewhat at fault for the state of our marriage, but I push the rogue thought aside.

I'm on a mission, and I can't allow myself to be distracted. I glide through the hallway as my feet ghost over the polished wood. It seems to absorb the light and my movements. My gaze flits from one shadow to the next as I hunt for any sign of life.

I've meticulously planned each step, each breath, to ensure that by now, the champagne's treacherous bubbles would have burst inside their veins, carrying the Rohypnol to its mark. The quiet reassures me that the drug has woven its incapacitating spell.

I move past the framed photographs on the wall—

their smiles mock me. My thumb brushes against the cool metal of the gun. I am close to them now, so very close. I can feel it in my bones.

There's no backing out now, not when I can almost taste the vindication that awaits at the end of this nightmarish path I've been forced to tread.

My hand is a vise around the gun as I edge toward the living room, each step deliberate and silent. I pause at the threshold, listening to any sounds of life, but there is only more silence.

Adrenaline surges, and with it, I imagine how I will find their unconscious bodies at any moment. My syringe to the champagne bottle—evidence of my perfect crime. With the pair of them helpless, I will use Lucas's own hand to grip the gun. It must be convincing, a crime of passion so intense that no one would doubt its authenticity. I must make sure the evidence tells the story I want: Lucas, the spurned lover, is unable to control his rage when Victoria tries to sell their illicit ties.

It has to be perfect, undeniable, as I consider the gun's placement and the shot's angle. The staging of this final act must be meticulous. The gunshot residue on Lucas's hand will be the silent witness to my fabrication, the unspoken testimony that will damn him and exonerate me.

I've never done anything like this, and the unknowns rattle through my mind. If I shoot Victoria and then turn the gun on Lucas for what appears to be a self-inflicted wound, will the jarring pain be enough to wake her? While I desperately cling to the hope I will be the last person she sees as her life slips away, I'm certain the neighbors will call the police when they hear the shots. I can't linger. I have to set the scene. As much as I desperately desire for Victoria to look into my eyes as she takes her final breath, I can't lose sight of my objective. I must fire the two fatal shots and then abruptly make my exit.

I steel my nerves, ready to transform the quiet space before me into a scene of orchestrated violence. I inch closer toward the kitchen, and the muted glow casts a soft light on the open bottle of champagne. My eyes flicker when I notice half the bottle is gone. A wave of relief washes over me as the reality settles in that the two took the bait.

But before I can revel in this anticipated confirmation, a floorboard groans behind me, slicing through the silence like a warning shot. Every muscle in my body tenses. I'm confident I haven't made a sound; the Rohypnol should have taken care of any resistance. None of this makes sense, but I know I heard it.

Someone is here. Someone is awake.

Time slows down, each millisecond stretching out as I pivot on my heel. But as my eyes start to register the shadow looming behind me, a blunt force crashes into the back of my head. Pain explodes in a blinding white flash, and my thoughts scatter like shards of glass.

The world spins, the darkness enveloping me like a suffocating blanket. Everything goes black.

PART TWO

DETECTIVE MARIA SANCHEZ

TWELVE

MARIA

I pull up to the luxurious and modern home, the fluttering yellow tape a stark contrast against the meticulously manicured lawn. My gaze sweeps over the scene—chaos in a place of order. I take a deep breath and step out of my unmarked car, slipping past the barrier that separates the everyday world from this bubble of tragedy.

Several members of the press gathered outside notice my presence and rush forward, trying to ask if I know what has happened inside. I ignore their questions as I flash my badge to one of the officers manning the police tape.

The sharp scent of fresh-cut grass mixes with something metallic in the air, a hint of blood not yet cleansed. I slip the chain that my badge is hanging from around my neck as I climb the steps to the picturesque home. The front porch has modern furniture, but the decor is minimalistic.

Nodding at an officer posted at the front entrance, my eyes quickly fix themselves on the doorbell camera. I make a note to make sure we download any footage it may have captured before I pass through the oversized doorway and down the modern hallway. As I near the kitchen, there are stairs to my left. At the base of the stairs is my victim—a man who appears to be in his forties. The coroner is busy at work with the body, so I move around them into the living room area off the kitchen.

My eyes land on a woman slumped against the arm of the oversized white sectional. A cotton dress that had once been white, now marred by the evening's events, hangs off her frame. Her face is pale, her eyes glassy, and she feels lost in some void only she can see.

On the other side of the room, a young man paces frantically. A paramedic is trying to attend to him, but he continually pulls his hand away, obviously agitated.

"Sir, please," the paramedic pleads as he follows the man back and forth. "I need to check your vitals."

"My vitals! My vitals?" He gasps frantically. "I can tell you exactly how my vitals are. My heart is beating out of my fucking chest because I just found a dead guy."

"Sir," I begin. The young man pauses his pacing and looks in my direction. "My name is Detective Maria Sanchez. Are you the one who made the call this morning?"

"Yes, yes, that was me," the young man stammers as he approaches me with hasty steps. His eyes are wide with panic, and his hands tremble at his sides. "It's so fucking messed up. I-I-I woke up and my head was pounding out of my skull. That's when I found him . . . like that," he utters, pointing a shaky finger toward the stairs where the lifeless body is.

Detective Sanchez studies him carefully, noting the genuine distress etched into his expression, but her years of experience have taught her to tread cautiously, even with those who seem innocent. "Is this your home?"

"What?" He seems confused by my question as he shakes his head. "No, of course not."

"It's my home," the woman perched on the sofa replies softly. "I'm Victoria McAllister and that man—" Her eyes dart in the direction of the victim. The words catch in her throat as she attempts to continue, but fails.

"That's her husband," the young man blurts out.

"I see," I respond to the interesting detail. I turn my attention back to the young man. "And you are?"

"Oh, I'm Lucas. Lucas Flynn. I work for Mr. McAllister—I mean, I did." As he says the words, his eyes flitter over toward the corpse at the base of the stairs.

"It's nice to meet you, Lucas Flynn," I reply in a tender voice meant to disarm the young man. "Can you tell me why you woke up at your boss's house?"

Lucas runs a hand through his disheveled hair, his breaths coming in ragged gasps. "I don't fucking know." The panic returns with a vengeance, and then suddenly, he is doubled over, fighting to catch his breath. The paramedic who had been attempting to assist him earlier rushes to his side.

Taking Lucas by the arm, the paramedic tells me he needs to get him to the hospital to have him checked out thoroughly. The paramedics look at each other and I notice the other one is taking Victoria's vitals. The one tending to Lucas informs the rest of the room that they are taking him to the ambulance.

Lucas stands upright before he is shakily assisted toward the exit, where the ambulance waits on the street. I turn toward the woman, who seems once again lost in her own world.

"Ma'am?" My voice slices through the frenzied whispers of uniformed officers and the soft murmurs of the crowd that have begun to gather beyond the perimeter. No response.

"Mrs. McAllister?" I try again, softer this time. Still nothing. The fragility in her posture tugs at something inside me, but I push it down. Emotion has no place here, not when answers hide beneath the surface.

"Detective Maria Sanchez," I announce, stepping into her line of sight, badge in hand for her to see. "I'm going to need to ask you some questions."

Her eyes flicker to mine, the blank stare of someone burdened with too much. I wait for a nod, a word, any sign of permission to proceed. The silence stretches between us.

"May I?" I prompt gently. A flicker of understanding dances behind her eyes, and she gives a near imperceptible nod.

"Thank you," I murmur, pulling out my notebook.

I watch as Victoria blinks. Her gaze slowly lifts to meet mine, and she stares with a mouth agape as if the world around her has shifted into an alien landscape. "It doesn't make sense," she whispers at last.

"What doesn't make sense, Mrs. McAllister?" I ask.

She swallows hard. A hint of a polite smile is all she manages to muster as she looks at me and says, "Victoria."

I nod. "Victoria," I mimic. "You were saying something doesn't make sense. What do you mean?"

She shakes her head. "He shouldn't be here."

"Your husband? Is that who you mean? Or are you talking about Mr. Flynn?" I attempt to clarify.

Her gaze fixes on me as she explains, "Jason. His business partner picked him up yesterday and took him to the airport. He's supposed to be at a conference in San Francisco." Her head briefly turns toward the body before looking away again. "But there he is. I don't understand."

"I see. I know this is difficult, but I need to understand what happened here," I continue as the paramedics tending to Victoria begin to pack their equipment back into their bags. "Can you think of anyone who might want to harm your husband?"

She blinks again, slower this time. Her lips part, but the words seem trapped behind the shock. When she finally speaks again, it's with a breathy quality, fragile as glass. "Everyone . . . Everyone loved Jason. He . . . he didn't have enemies in his personal life."

"What about outside his personal life?" I inquire softly, encouraging her to continue.

"His business?" she continues after a moment, her voice gaining a fraction of strength. "I don't know about that. I know a lot was happening there right now. He was close to some sort of acquisition deal or something. You'd have to ask his partner. Declan would know more about that side of things."

"Thank you, Victoria. That's very helpful," I reassure her, making a mental note to follow up with this Declan character.

"Detective," the paramedic interrupts. "I really need to get her to the hospital so they can do a thorough checkup."

I look up at the young woman in her pressed uniform. She barely looks old enough to drive, let alone work as an emergency paramedic. However, she is the picture of professionalism. "Were samples taken from both Mr. Flynn and Mrs. McAllister?"

The girl nods. "Yes, ma'am. They will be handed over to the hospital for the tox screens."

"Thank you. I only have a few more questions for Victoria before I let her go with you," I add as I shift gears, hoping to piece together the timeline leading up to the crime. "Victoria, I saw some champagne on the kitchen counter when I came in. Were you and Lucas—"

She doesn't wait for my insinuation. "We were celebrating."

"Celebrating?" I attempt to clarify.

"I've been helping Lucas study for his real estate licensing exam," she explains.

"Oh really? You're a real estate agent?" I question.

"I was," she sighs. "Before I married Jason. But after we got married, he said he didn't think it was good for his image for me to work anymore."

"Oh wow, that must have been hard for you to give up," I reply, wondering if I had just stumbled into a possible motive.

Her eyes flicker with a spark of recognition, a semblance of clarity cutting through the fog. She chuffs, "No, that wasn't hard. My husband made sure I had everything I ever wanted. He loved me."

"That's wonderful," I reply, feeling the sharpness of her words. "Was Jason here for the celebration?" I probe gently.

She looks at me with suspicion in her eyes now. "I told you Jason was supposed to be at a conference in San Francisco."

"That's right," I quickly correct myself as I can see her walls going up. "You did say that. I'm sorry." I watch her struggle to maintain composure. I need to tread carefully, or I'll lose her trust before we even start. "And your husband, how did he react when he learned about these study sessions?"

Victoria looks away, a muscle twitching in her jaw. "He didn't know," she murmurs, almost too quiet to catch. "It was nice to get back into that world, even if it was just as a tutor. I wanted to tell him, but Lucas was worried Jason wouldn't want me to help him. I didn't think . . ."

"Think what?"

"That it mattered." Her gaze snaps back to me, defensive. "It was innocent, Detective Sanchez."

"Secrets have a way of becoming something else, even if that wasn't the intent." I keep my tone neutral. "You can understand why someone might see you not wanting to tell your husband, which makes it seem a little suspect."

"No, I can't, Detective Sanchez, because I loved my husband, and he loved me," she retorts defiantly.

"Then why not tell him?"

"Lucas said he thought my husband wouldn't want him to keep working for him if he knew he planned to leave eventually." She answers before confidently adding, "I know what you're insinuating, and I can tell you that as far as our marriage, he wouldn't have cared. Our marriage wasn't built on jealousy."

I study Victoria's face, searching for any flicker of deception. Her eyes hold mine, fierce and unyielding.

"I wasn't insinuating anything. I hope you know I want to figure out how this happened to your husband as much as you do," I assure her.

"Good," Victoria confirms. She swipes at a tear that threatens to escape.

Before I can ask another question, the paramedic steps forward. "I'm sorry, Detective Sanchez. We really need to take Mrs. McAllister and Mr. Flynn to the hospital now," she says firmly.

Victoria seems to shrink back at her words.

"Of course," I acknowledge. "Victoria, I would like to continue with these questions once you finish your checkup." I slip her my business card and ask her to reach out once she is discharged.

"Thank you, I will," she whispers.

I watch as Victoria exits. Her eyes are fixed on her husband until she makes her way past him at the far end of the hallway. I hear a whimper from her in the distance and wonder if it's genuine or for my benefit. Something happened here last night that left a man dead, and nobody present seems to have a clue.

"Detective?" One of my officers approaches, flipping through pages on a clipboard. I glance at his name tag.

"Yes, what is it, Officer Simpson?"

"I thought you would want to know that we took a sample from both Mr. Flynn and Mrs. McAllister for gunshot residue," he explains.

"Let's hear it," I say, tucking a strand of my raven-colored hair behind my ear, my focus sharp.

"Negative on both," he reports.

"Thank you, that's good to know." I glance toward the ambulance, watching as they load Victoria and Lucas inside. "Make sure you send a copy of those results to my attention at the precinct."

"Will do."

These findings do not exonerate the pair present at Jason McAllister's demise. They would not have been the first to wear gloves and change their clothes after committing a crime, but it does help remove some suspicion.

I pivot on my heel and turn toward the coroner, who is finishing up his inspection of the body. "Hey, Hal," I murmur as I approach. "How's it looking?"

"Looking like a dead guy," he answers nonchalantly.

I chuckle at Hal's signature dark humor amid the grim scene. "Anything out of the ordinary?" I press, knowing that Hal's observations often unearth crucial details.

He straightens, adjusting his glasses as he turns to face me. "Single gunshot wound to the chest," he states, his tone all business. "Close range. No signs of struggle, so it was most likely unexpected. Time of death estimated to be between eleven and two a.m."

Eleven and two a.m.—a window of time that would need to be narrowed down. "Any defensive wounds on the victim?"

Hal shakes his head. "No defensive wounds." He pauses, his gaze flickering toward the staircase. "But there was something sort of strange."

"What's that?" I ask.

"He took a pretty significant knock to the head. I'll have to complete the autopsy first to make sure it was the gunshot to the chest that killed him and not the blow to the head," he explains.

"Could he have hit his head falling after he was shot?"

Hal shakes his head. "There's no sign that he hit his head on the stairs or anything else, so it had to be something else. I should be able to get a mold of the wound for you."

"Perfect," I reply. "Keep me posted."

My gaze roams across the lifeless form of Jason McAllister sprawled near the bottom of the staircase, an undignified end for a man who clearly had built quite the life for himself.

My focus narrows to Jason's twisted posture. Did he land that way, or was he positioned? I take a step closer, crouching down, eyeing the angle of the bullet wound. "How long on the report, Hal?" I ask as he packs up his gear.

He pauses and chuffs in my direction. "When have you known me to reply anything besides the standard two weeks?"

I sigh a heavy breath. "Fair enough. Based on this zip code, the chief will be breathing down both our necks."

"Zip codes don't come into play for me," he says dismissively as he grabs the body bag a few steps away and lays it out on the floor.

Rising so Hal can finish his job, I move to the front of the home and glance through the windows. There they are—vultures perched in their news vans, cameras already trained on the house. They're ready to broadcast this tragedy to every household hungry for scandal.

"Dammit." I exhale sharply, pressing my fingertips to the bridge of my nose. This case is about to become a circus, and keeping a lid on it won't be easy. I look back at Jason's body. I've dealt with high-profile cases like this before. The media frenzy outside is a beast that will feed on every detail, factual or not, and I need to stay ahead of it or answer for it to the chief.

"Make sure you keep them back," I instruct the nearest officer, gesturing toward the press. "And get screens up around the entrance. I don't want a single shot of the body making it onto the evening news."

"Right away, Detective Sanchez."

I give a final survey of the crime scene, etching every detail into my memory—the position of the body, the scent of iron mixed with expensive cologne. I watch the scene processing agents working tirelessly, collecting various fingerprints from throughout the home.

"Time to get to work," I say under my breath, my resolve hardening. I have a killer to catch, and no amount of flashing cameras or sensational headlines will stand in my way.

Pulling out my phone, I punch in the message with rapid-fire taps. Bishop, where are you? My thumbs hover over the screen as I wait.

Caught up at home, he replies, and I can almost hear his nonchalant shrug through the text.

I told you this case is high-profile, I fire back.

Sounds like you've got it handled. See you at the precinct.

His response makes my blood boil. Handled? I stifle the urge to throw my phone. Ever since I got saddled with William Bishop, I have basically been flying solo. If someone were to ask me to describe my new partner in a couple words, they would be incompetent and lazy.

I slip my phone back into my pocket, feeling the ache of frustration that has become a near-constant companion since I started working with Bishop. The memory of my previous partner, Eddie, seeps in. A good cop and a true partner. His death left a void no one could fill, especially not Bishop, with his retirement countdown and lackadaisical approach to the job. I work alone now, effectively if not officially. It's better this way. No distractions, no disappointments, and nobody to let down like I did Eddie.

THIRTEEN

MARIA

The blaring alarm clock slices through the stillness of my bedroom. A shrill reminder that today, like every day, begins before the sun is up. I slap the snooze button. Reluctantly, I force my eyes open, squinting against the soft glow of the digital numbers that read 5:00 a.m.—a time most reasonable people would still consider night.

I roll out of bed, my feet hitting the cold floor with a jolt that travels up my spine. In the bathroom, I face the mirror. The woman who stares back at me looks about as weary as I feel—dark circles under her eyes stand testament to nights spent piecing together puzzles of human malice. I reach for the faucet, twist it, and let the water run until it's ice cold. Then, cupping my hands, I gather some and splash it onto my face.

Standing before the open closet, I inspect my available wardrobe choices. After quick consideration, I opt for a simple yet professional outfit. Going sensibly, as always, I choose a crisp white blouse paired with a tailored navy blazer and black slacks.

Downstairs in the kitchen, the smell of coffee permeates the air, beckoning me closer. I pour myself a cup, relishing in the warmth that seeps into my palms. Hurried footsteps approaching from the hallway break the silence.

"Mom, seriously? I can't believe you are still making me get up so damn early. I'm telling you I can get to school on my own," my daughter grumbles, her tone a blend of frustration and teenage defiance.

"Language," I say, reminding her with a mother's disapproving glare.

She huffs. "Oh my God. Do you realize how important sleep is for a growing teenager's mind? I miss out because you don't trust me and insist on dropping me off at Nana Maddie's at the crack of dawn."

"This is hardly the crack of dawn, Jordan," I reply dismissively. "And I told you, if you manage to stay out of trouble for six months, we can discuss it."

When faced with an inconvenient truth, her eyes narrow, a mirror image of her father.

"Whatever," she huffs as she crosses her arms. "Can I go to Dad's after school today?"

"Jordan." I keep my tone even despite the tightness in my throat. "You know we talked about this. He's too far out of the way for a school night." I grab two protein bars and toss her one, feeling compelled to justify my response further. "With everything going on right now at work, it's not the best time."

"That's always your excuse," she counters, her voice rising just enough to carry a sharp edge.

The remark stings more than I let it show. I take a deep breath and try to remember that as much as I loathe Marshall, he is still her father. "That's not fair. You know your dad doesn't have a car right now, so I have to pick you up on the way home from work. That means neither of us will get to bed at a decent time. I wish things were different, but this is how things have to be right now," I say softly, meeting her gaze.

Her shoulders slump in defeat, and she nods, though her disappointment is as clear as day. I reach out and grip her arm. It's a silent apology, an acknowledgment of the sacrifices she makes because of what I do. I take it as a win when she doesn't pull away.

"I know," she mutters, and I can hear the reluctant acceptance in her voice.

We step into the crisp morning air, the neighborhood beginning to stir from slumber. Climbing into the standard-issue detective car, I run through the list of mom questions I need to ask her as I drive her to my ex's mother's house while Jordan waits for the bus to arrive.

"Remember, you have a math test today," I remind her, voice soft but firm against the quiet hum of the waking world.

"Yeah, I studied with Dad last night over video chat," she replies, her tone carrying that teenage nonchalance.

As we drive, my mind starts to drift, leaving behind the domestic for the darker aspects of my work. Lucas.

The name echoes in my head. What does he know? Was he so agitated on the day I initially met him? Was he distraught over finding Jason McAllister's body, or was there a deeper reason for his uneasiness? Did he have something to do with the man's untimely death?

He isn't the only suspect who gnaws at me. Victoria. Her silence. If she had nothing to do with her husband's death, why wouldn't I have already heard from her?

"Mom?" My daughter's voice pulls me back, and I realize I've been sitting at a stoplight long after it turned green.

"Sorry, just thinking about work," I confess, offering her a smile. She nods, accustomed to my divided attention, the part of me always tangled up in unsolved cases.

"Will you be home for dinner?" she asks, hopeful yet guarded.

I want to promise yes and assure her that nothing will keep me from our evening routine. "I'll do my best," I say.

She smiles and accepts the answer for what it is—another compromise in a life full of them.

I pull up to Jordan's grandmother's house, and as she gets out of the car, I call after her, "Remember, make good choices." It's our daily mantra, one she knows by heart. She rolls her eyes, but a curve to her lips tells me she appreciates the routine.

"Will do, Detective Mom." She grins, slinging her backpack over her shoulder. "Catch the bad guys today?"

"Always trying," I reply with a wink. She doesn't look back, and I fight the urge to call out and hold her for a moment longer.

The precinct is not far, so I navigate the short drive on autopilot. Parking in my usual spot, I kill the engine and gather my badge and gun.

The glass doors glide open with a hush, ushering me into the buzz of the precinct. "Sanchez." Officer Clarke nods as I pass the front desk. Her voice anchors me back into this world of law and order.

"Morning." I return the greeting, my gaze sweeping across the room. Officers huddle over desks, and phones ring incessantly.

I stride to the corner of the bullpen and flick on the small desk lamp, casting a warm circle of light that pushes back the sterile glare of the overhead fluorescents. The precinct is a hive of activity, but I carve out a bubble of focus here at my desk.

I pull a stack of folders toward me, their contents ready to spill out with details of the dozens of cases I've meticulously annotated over the months. I shuffle them into order. Each is a story, an unanswered question, a life hanging in the balance. They deserve my attention, no matter how eager I am to meet with Lucas and pry open the secrets he's clutching tight.

I fill my morning hours with dozens of reports and calls, following up on leads from various cases, including ones that have long since gone cold. I cap my pen once I complete the last form and glance at the clock. The meeting with Lucas is looming and I need to navigate through it meticulously. But another puzzle demands attention—Victoria.

She hasn't called. That silence a persistent itch that no amount of paperwork can soothe. I've been patient, expecting her to reach out, but patience is a virtue that wears thin rather quickly when investigating the murder of one's husband.

I decide after my interview with Lucas, I'll call her. That way I will be armed with details from him that might spur her to be a bit more cooperative.

I push back from my desk, the chair wheels groaning softly in protest.

"Where are you headed in such a hurry?" Bishop asks from his cubicle next to me when he sees me stand.

"We have our interview with that kid from the McAllister murder," I remind him, not shielding the annoyance from my voice.

Bishop nods, rubbing a hand over his clean-shaven jaw. "Right, the kid who found the body. Think he knows more than he let on?"

I shrug slightly, grabbing my blazer from the back of my chair. "Hard to say."

Bishop raises an eyebrow, a silent question hanging between us. The McAllister murder has the entire precinct on edge ever since it hit the headlines. A high-profile couple, a gruesome crime scene, and a young and handsome employee at the residence at the time of the killing.

"You coming on this one?" I ask Bishop, trying not to assume anything when it comes to him.

"Of course I am, partner," he scoffs as if it shouldn't have even been a question.

As we approach the interrogation room, my mind races through possible scenarios. Lucas could be telling the truth; he woke up to find the body and then called the police. I'm still waiting on the results of the toxicology reports, but both Lucas and Victoria claim they were rendered unconscious before Jason arrived at the home.

We reach the interrogation room and find Lucas already escorted inside and waiting nervously. I watch him through the glass, his body tense and his fingers fidgeting with the hem of his shirt. Whatever secrets Lucas may have, I don't think it will be hard for me to pry them from him.

FOURTEEN

MARIA

I sit across from Lucas, the air in the interrogation room dense with tension. "Lucas," I begin, my voice steady and authoritative. "Thanks for coming in. This is my partner, Detective Bishop."

Lucas shifts uncomfortably in his chair, his eyes flitting between Detective Bishop and me. My partner nods in his direction as he sits next to me. "No problem," he mutters, his voice barely above a whisper. "But I'm not really sure I can help you much."

"Of course, you can help me. You were the one who discovered Mr. McAllister's body. If anyone can help us solve this case, it may be you," I assure him.

"It's just . . . well, I can't really think of anything that could be of any help," he stammers.

"You'd be surprised what people know that can help, but they don't even realize it," I assure him.

I watch as Lucas fidgets, his eyes avoiding mine. I try to get a read on him. Anyone would be uncomfortable sitting in an interrogation room across from two detectives, especially if they had recently woken up to find the corpse of their boss in the same room. I can't assume his jitteriness is anything out of the ordinary. Leaning closer, I outstretch a hand across the table to let him know I want to help. I must gain his trust from the beginning.

"I know this is hard, so how about we start with that night? Tell me everything you remember about that day that has anything to do with the McAllisters," I urge gently, watching for any flicker of hesitation in his eyes.

"Okay—um, well, I called Vic—Mrs. McAllister earlier in the day to tell her I had gotten the results of the exam," Lucas says.

"Is this the real estate exam you're talking about?" I attempt to clarify as Bishop sits quietly next to me.

Lucas nods. "Yeah, she has been so much help to me. She was the first person I wanted to tell when I found out."

I nod, noting the sincerity in his voice. "That's understandable. It sounds like she means a lot to you. What happened next after you informed Mrs. McAllister about passing the exam?"

Lucas takes a deep breath, his eyes distant as if he's replaying the events in his mind. "We decided to meet up later that day for a celebratory drink."

"And where did you go for that drink?" I press.

"Oh, well, she said that her husband had just picked her up a bottle of her favorite champagne the night before, so it was perfect timing," he explains.

"So you went to her house for the drink?" Bishop asks.

I glance at Detective Bishop, who jots down some notes on his notepad when Lucas confirms this detail. He clears his throat, shifting in his seat once more. "I also brought her some chocolates to thank her for all her help."

"Chocolates?" Bishop questions. "Isn't that kind of a romantic gift?"

Lucas hesitates, moistening his lips with a nervous flick of his tongue. "What? No! I mean it can be, but it's not what you're thinking."

"And what are we thinking exactly?" my partner presses. I flash him a sharp look, hoping he can sense my trying to tell him to back off. He's pushing the boy too hard, too fast.

"I wasn't having an affair with her, if that's what you're trying to say," Lucas snaps. "I have a girlfriend who I love very much. I plan to ask her to marry me—I wouldn't do that to her."

"Nobody is trying to insinuate anything. We're all just trying to figure out what happened to your boss," I assure him. "So you show up with the chocolates. What time was that?"

"I don't know. Maybe nine o'clock," he answers.

"Wow, that's pretty late for a celebratory drink between friends, right?" Bishop chuffs.

My head snaps in my partner's direction, and my eyes grow wide as my nostrils flare. "Detective Bishop,"

I interject firmly, "why don't we let Lucas finish telling us what happened after he arrived."

Lucas visibly relaxes at my intervention and continues, "Well, we had a drink or two. And then I remember feeling really tired all of a sudden."

"Okay, and what happened next?" I prompt gently, urging him to recount the events of that fateful night.

His brow furrows as he struggles to recollect. "The next thing I remember is waking up with a pounding headache and finding Mr. McAllister . . . dead. I told you I couldn't help you at all."

Detective Bishop looks up from his notes with a curious expression. "What about Mrs. McAllister? Was she awake when you passed out?"

Lucas furrows his brow, trying to remember. "She . . . I don't know if she fell asleep at the same time, but she was asleep across from me when I woke up."

"Are you certain?" I ask.

He nods confidently. "I had to shake her awake."

"Good, you're doing good," I assure him. "Now, Mrs. McAllister told me that you didn't want Mr. McAllister to find out that she was helping you. Why is that?"

Lucas shifts in his chair, a nervous sheen breaking out on his forehead. "I . . . I was afraid if he found out my plans, he would ruin my opportunities before I even had a chance."

"Why exactly would he do that? Was there a reason your boss wouldn't want you to pursue another career path?"

Lucas scoffs. "Not if he were a normal human, but nothing about Jason McAllister was normal."

As Lucas's words hang in the air, tension fills the room. His eyes dart nervously between Detective Bishop, me, and the one-way mirror as if expecting someone to burst in at any moment. I lean back in my chair, studying his expression for any signs of deception or fear.

"What do you mean by that?" I prod gently.

Lucas swallows hard, his Adam's apple bobbing visibly. "Nothing—I mean…well, he wasn't the kind you want to cross."

Detective Bishop leans forward, his tone more serious now. "Are you saying that your boss had a history of violence?"

Lucas hesitates. "Not exactly . . . He never liked it when things didn't go his way, that's all. I don't mean to speak ill of—well, you know, but he's a big shot in this town. He's used to people doing anything to get the chance to work for him, and here I was, newer to the company and already looking for an exit."

"I see," I interject quickly when I see Bishop start to open his mouth. "Is that what happened that night? Did Mr. McAllister find out you were planning to leave the company and had asked his wife to help you? Did he become volatile? We would understand if you were simply trying to protect yourself or Mrs. McAllister."

Lucas's eyes grow wide at the shift in my questioning, and his mouth falls open. "Wait, what? You think I did this?"

"Look, just fess up to it now, kid, and a judge will go way easier on you," Bishop grunts as he leans back in his chair and pats his oversized belly.

Lucas's face pales, aghast at the accusation. He stammers, "No, I didn't do anything! I would never harm Mr. McAllister or anyone else!" His hands tremble as he looks desperately between Detective Bishop and me, seeking some glimmer of understanding.

I raise a hand to halt Bishop. "Lucas, take a deep breath. We're not accusing you of anything just yet. We need to understand all sides of the story. Tell us what happened after you woke up and found Mr. McAllister."

Lucas swallows hard, visibly relieved that I'm giving him a chance to clarify. "I-I panicked," he admits, nervously running a hand through his hair. "I thought about running out of there, but then I saw Victoria lying there, and I didn't want her to wake up and be all alone and find her husband like that, not after she helped me. So, like I said, I shook her, and we called 911 right away, and then . . . I don't remember much after that. The paramedics arrived, the police . . ."

"Did Mrs. McAllister say anything to you about her husband before the police arrived?" I question.

He shakes his head. "She went to go check on him, and I told her she shouldn't touch him, but she said she needed to make sure he wasn't still alive."

"Is that how she got the blood on her dress?" I inquire.

Lucas licks his dry lips before replying with a shaky voice, "Yeah, I mean, I think that's when it happened. She went to him, and that's when she must have gotten the blood on her." He's clearly distressed by the memory.

I watch Lucas closely, sensing his turmoil as he recounts that dreadful night. Bishop leans back in his chair, scribbling notes on a pad before him, his expression unreadable.

I exchange a glance with Bishop before turning back to Lucas. "Do you think Mrs. McAllister could have been involved in her husband's death?"

Lucas's eyes widen in shock at the suggestion. "No! No way! She loved him! She wouldn't—"

"Lucas," I interrupt. "We need to consider all possibilities in this case. Your account of that night is crucial in helping us get to the truth."

Lucas runs a hand through his hair anxiously, clearly torn between loyalty to Victoria and the need to be honest with the detectives. His eyes dart back and forth.

After a moment of tense silence, he finally speaks, his voice low and trembling. "I . . . I don't know. She was so frantic when she found him . . . I can't imagine she would've . . ." He's unable to finish the thought.

I lean forward, my elbows planted firmly on the cool metal table, feeling the sharp edges of determination etching lines into my arms. My eyes narrow as I scrutinize Lucas, searching for the cracks in his carefully constructed façade. "You're doing so good. Victoria would be so proud of how much you have helped us so far."

I catch Bishop rolling his eyes from the corner of my eye. He rocks forward, and the room jumps when my partner slams his hands on the table. "Were you fucking her?"

"Wh-who? M-Mrs. McAllister?" Lucas stammers. "I told you. She was just helping me pass the exam."

"And there has never been anything more between you and her? Anything at all? And be careful how you answer because we will find out," Bishop warns. I consider silencing him but then think better of it. Perhaps Lucas needs a little pressure.

For a moment, he's silent, his lips parting as if to speak, yet no words come forth. Then, with a sigh that seems to deflate him, he speaks. "No, nothing like that. But . . . there was this one time—we were at a hotel restaurant for lunch and a study session."

"Go on," I press, sensing the reluctance woven into his every syllable.

He continues, his voice full of apprehension. "She was . . . affectionate. Hugs, and she—well, when we were leaving and standing on the sidewalk, she kissed me on the lips."

My eyebrows shoot up, but I keep my voice calm and measured. "And how did you respond to her affections?"

"Look, I didn't—" He pauses. "I mean, I didn't reciprocate. It caught me off guard."

"Did she say anything about it afterward?" I probe, watching the battle play out across his features—the need to protect her warring with the urge to save himself.

"I guess she could sense that it caught me off guard a little, and she said she's very affectionate by nature," he finally murmurs. "She told me she hoped I wouldn't misinterpret her actions."

"And did you believe her?" I ask as he avoids my gaze.

He takes a moment, his eyes shifting as he struggles to form his next words. "I did." His voice is barely above a whisper. "I thought . . . I thought she was trying to be friendly." He looks up at me, his eyes pleading for understanding. "I really did."

I nod slowly, absorbing his words. It's clear that Lucas is torn between his loyalty to Victoria and the weight of the truth he's carrying. "Thank you for being honest with us, Lucas." I reach out to touch his arm briefly to reassure him.

He flinches slightly at the contact but doesn't pull away. "I didn't want any of this to happen," he mumbles, almost to himself.

"I believe you," I tell him firmly, though it's clear from his body language he's hiding something else. Cooperation can make a world of difference in cases like this, so despite the fact I don't fully trust him to tell me everything, I'm not ready to push him too hard yet. "I mean it when I say you've been very helpful. We may need to talk again later. Is that okay?"

He nods even though he really has no choice in the matter.

I stand, the metal legs of the chair scraping softly against the floor. My movements are deliberate, a signal that this interview is over—for now.

He watches me. "Detective Sanchez?" His voice cracks, brittle as thin ice. "What . . . what happens now?"

I pause as I wait for my partner to stand as well then glance down at Lucas. "Well, for right now, you are free to go, and we keep digging until we get to the bottom of this."

As soon as we exit the room, Bishop asks if I'm up for lunch. Glancing at my watch, I grunt that it's only ten o'clock, and he revises his suggestion to breakfast.

"No thanks, I'm good," I tell him before we part ways.

I settle into the worn fabric of my desk chair, the groan of its springs a familiar protest. I lay out the notes from Lucas's interview in front of me. His words, once hanging in the air of the interrogation room, now lie flat and lifeless on paper.

Lucas's denial of an affair with Victoria doesn't sit right. It's too clean, too rehearsed. He's not the loyal boyfriend he portrays himself to be; there's ambition in his veins, a desire for more than what's rightfully his. But does that ambition stretch as far as murder?

The mention of chocolates and champagne nags at me. A thank you, he said. An innocuous gesture turned sinister by what followed. Lucas waking up with a migraine; the scene he stumbled upon—Victoria unconscious and Jason McAllister dead. It sounds like a setup, a scene crafted to incriminate. But who stands to gain from this twisted play?

I sift through the timeline again. Victoria's affection at the hotel restaurant and the unexpected kiss—do they paint a picture of a woman not wholly satisfied in her marriage, or was it innocent, as Lucas claimed?

My phone buzzes with an incoming message, breaking my concentration. It's from the chief. He's requesting I come and chat with him about the case I'm working on. I'm working on a dozen different cases at the moment. Still, I assume he's probably referring to the McAllister's because it's high-profile.

"Right away," I reply and stand from my desk.

I have never been good at playing politics, not like the chief. It's like he was born to rub elbows with politicians and wealthy donors. A man like him was made to sit in his seat when it came to a city like LA.

I make my way down the familiar corridors of the police station, nodding at colleagues as I pass by. The chief's office looms ahead, its dark wooden door a stark contrast against the white walls. I knock once and enter without waiting for a response.

"Detective Sanchez, please take a seat." The chief gestures toward a chair opposite his desk, his expression unreadable.

I oblige, folding my hands neatly in my lap as I face him. "You wanted to see me, sir?"

The chief leans back in his chair, steepling his fingers

beneath his chin. "Thank you for coming so quickly. I've wanted to speak with you since I assigned you the McAllister case. It's getting a lot of attention, you know." His sharp gaze is assessing.

I nod slowly, keeping my tone neutral. "Yes, sir, I noticed."

He studies me for a moment before continuing. "I trust you're handling it with the delicacy it requires."

"I'm handling it with as much care as I handle all my cases, sir," I reply evenly.

"Any suspects yet?"

I hold his gaze steadily, giving away nothing. "It's still early in the investigation, sir. We are exploring all possible leads."

The chief leans forward. "You know, Mr. McAllister was a close friend of the mayor."

"I didn't know that, sir." I keep my tone respectful but firm.

He nods. "He would like me to keep him apprised of the investigation."

"Well, like I said, sir, there isn't much to report back right now. Neither of the individuals in the home at the time the body was discovered had GSR on their hands. For now, though, it will be three or four weeks before I have the autopsy and toxicology reports back. I plan to focus on interviewing people who knew the victim and look for a possible motive."

The chief's expression is unreadable. "I made a couple of calls this morning to put a rush on the reports. You won't have to wait so long."

"Sir?" The word slips out in response to his statement. In my entire career, I have never had the chief step in to rush the results of an autopsy. It is simply something that isn't done. But here he is and without any prompting from me.

"I know you understand the importance of this case, but I also need you to know that there are . . . external pressures at play here," he says carefully, weighing each word.

My gut clenches at his words. External pressures could mean anything from political interests to influential people pulling strings behind the scenes.

"I need your full cooperation in this matter, Detective," the chief continues.

"Of course, sir," I reply automatically, though a flicker of unease dances in the pit of my stomach.

I leave the chief's office with a sense of foreboding settling over me like a heavy shroud. The rush on the autopsy and toxicology reports, the mention of external pressures. As I walk back to my desk, my face flushes hot with frustration. Where were the rushes for the hundreds of other cases I have worked on in my career? The cases were full of victims and their loved ones who didn't have forces that could tip the scales of justice.

The last place I want to be is inside the walls of this precinct at the moment. I grab my purse and text Bishop that I plan to go to Haven and interview the victim's coworkers, asking if he would like to come along.

Busy. You got this. His reply flashes across my

screen. I'm not surprised by the response, and I hate to say that part of me is relieved. Bishop is sloppy and unpredictable regarding interviews, so I prefer to handle them on my own.

As I leave the police station and enter the harsh sunlight, my thoughts shift to Victoria. Haven may be my first stop today, but if I don't hear from her by the time I leave there, she will be my next one.

FIFTEEN

MARIA

I exit the elevator and enter through the large glass doors of Haven's offices. A petite brunette sits at the front desk, speaking in a polite voice to someone on the other end of the line. Considering the place recently lost its CEO, I'm not sure what I expected to find, but there aren't any obvious signs of grief hanging over the space.

The receptionist glances up at me and offers me a soft smile. A moment later, she redirects her call and greets me.

"Hello, welcome to Haven AI Solutions. May I help you?"

I nod and present my badge to her. "I'm Detective Sanchez. I'm here to see Declan Harris," I reply.

"Is he expecting you?" she asks with a curious expression.

"No, but I am here to discuss Jason McAllister with him," I explain.

Her face contorts into one filled with horror. "That is so terrible what happened to him, isn't it?"

I nod solemnly in agreement. "Did you know him well?"

She considers my question for a moment before responding. "Not really. I've only been here a few months, but he always seemed nice when I spoke to him." She picks up the phone before adding, "Let me check and see if Mr. Harris is available."

After a brief conversation, she hangs up the phone and tells me that Mr. Harris will be right with me. Moments later, a tall man with salt-and-pepper hair approaches us. His demeanor is calm and collected, his expression neutral.

"Detective Sanchez?" he asks with an outstretched hand. "I'm Declan Harris."

I greet him and explain that I have a few questions for him.

"Of course. Please follow me," he adds, gesturing for me to accompany him into his office.

We enter the modestly decorated space, and I settle into a chair across from his desk. He moves around to sit on his desk chair, and as I wait for him, I dive straight into the heart of the matter. "Mr. Harris, I hope you believe me when I tell you I'm here to find out who did this to your business partner. Maybe you could tell me who might want Mr. McAllister dead."

Declan's unwavering gaze meets mine. He considers my words carefully before responding, "I considered Jason a friend, but anyone who knew him also knew that he wasn't the easiest man to get along with."

"Are you saying he had a lot of enemies?" I press.

His brow creases as he responds, "I'm saying I may have been one of his only friends, and even that is probably being a little generous in definition."

"That doesn't really answer my question."

Declan leans back in his chair with a thoughtful expression on his face. "Detective Sanchez, I can't say for certain who would want Jason dead. He was a complicated man with complicated relationships."

As I study Declan's face for any hints of deception, I notice a flicker of something in his eyes. Was it guilt? Regret? Or was I just reading too much into it?

Deciding to change tactics, I asked, "Do you have any idea why a company employee was at Jason's house the night he was killed?"

Declan pauses for a moment as if weighing his words carefully. "I don't like to speak on matters I don't have all the facts on," he replies. His polite and practiced smile doesn't reach those guarded eyes.

I can feel the tension in the room as Declan easily avoids my question. His reluctance to provide any details only adds to my suspicion. However, I decide to push a bit further.

"Did Mr. McAllister ever express any concerns to you about his personal life or relationships?" I inquire, watching Declan closely for even the slightest change in his demeanor.

Declan leans forward, his hands clasped on the

desk, and finally meets my gaze directly. "Jason was a private man, Detective Sanchez. He kept his personal affairs close to the chest, as they say," he replies cryptically. "But yes, I knew he had concerns about his marriage's health."

"I see. So did Mr. McAllister believe his wife was having an affair?" I ask cautiously.

At the mention of Victoria, I see a flash of something in Declan's eyes, too quick for me to identify before it's gone. He clears his throat before responding carefully, "I suppose since he's gone, I'm not betraying his trust, but I do believe Jason had hired a private investigator to follow Victoria."

As Declan watches me with expectant eyes, I fold my hands in my lap, a barrier of sorts. "And do you know if he uncovered anything?"

Declan takes a deep breath, his gaze fixed on a point just over my shoulder as he considers his reply. "I don't know for sure what Jason found out," he admits slowly, "but he was convinced that Victoria was seeing someone behind his back."

"And do you think he was right?" I question.

"Honestly, I don't know. Victoria never seemed like the cheating type, but who knows what being married to a man like Jason could drive a person to do." As soon as the words leave his lips, I can tell he regrets them. He quickly adds, "No matter what, Victoria could never hurt Jason. I could tell she knew about all his infidelities, but she stuck by him."

I perk up at the revelation. "So Mr. McAllister

wasn't the faithful kind?" A pang of sympathy grows in my gut for Victoria, and I try my best to extinguish it. Despite the fact I was once married to a serial cheater, there is no room for emotions when it comes to my job. I can't let this new detail cloud my judgment.

Declan's eyes flicker with mixed emotions, perhaps regret or even relief that the conversation is finally moving away from him and his connections to the case. "Jason was . . . complicated, Detective. He had his flaws like we all do," he replies vaguely as if trying to distance himself from any potential suspicion.

I study Declan's reaction closely, analyzing every word and movement in my mind. His composed demeanor doesn't quite match the unease in his eyes. It's as if he's a chess player carefully calculating his next move, guarding his pieces closely.

As his words hang heavy in the air, I decide to change tactics once more. "Mr. Harris, did Jason ever talk to you about any threats he might have received? Any enemies within or outside the company?"

Declan's mask slips for just a moment before he composes himself with practiced ease. "Threats? Not that I'm aware of. Haven AI Solutions operates in a competitive industry, but I don't believe Jason ever mentioned feeling personally threatened by anyone." His tone is almost too smooth, as if he's reciting lines from a script.

"So there is a chance this could have been a work-related attack?"

Declan chuckles. "I mean, I suppose anything is

possible, but it's not like the movies, Detective Sanchez." I stiffen at his condescending remark.

"Mrs. McAllister told me that Jason wasn't supposed to be in town at the time of his murder. She said that you had picked him up for the airport," I say more to remind the smug man sitting across from me that even he is a suspect and should perhaps consider his words carefully.

Declan's demeanor shifts imperceptibly at my mention of Victoria. Still, he quickly recovers, a mask of indifference settling over his features again. "Yes, I picked him up, and he flew to San Francisco with me."

"If he was in San Francisco with you, can you explain to me how he ended up shot later that night in his home back in LA?" I inquire, my gaze fixed on him.

"I wish I could. He made an appearance that night at a welcome event for the conference and then complained he wasn't feeling great and was going to turn in early."

"And what time was that?"

"Jesus, I don't know," Declan replies gruffly, my questions starting to ruffle him. "Maybe six or seven."

"Then how on earth was he with you at six or seven, and then five hours later, he is getting shot in his home in LA?" I question, observing how uncomfortable my questions seem to be making the man.

Declan shifts in his chair, a frustrated glint in his eyes as he struggles to find an explanation. Despite the chill in the room, I can see beads of sweat forming on his forehead. His calm demeanor is cracking under the weight of my interrogation, revealing the cracks in his facade.

"I-I don't know, Detective Sanchez," he stammers, his voice barely above a whisper. "It doesn't make sense. He told me he was going to put his phone on Do Not Disturb and would see me for our pitch meetings the next day. When he didn't show up, I figured he had lied to me and went out partying."

"Is that something Mr. McAllister would often do when the two of you traveled?"

"What?" He grunts in surprise. "No . . . I mean, sometimes, I guess. When he needed to blow off steam."

I already knew Jason was in San Francisco. In fact, the hotel staff had recovered his phone in his room, and it was being shipped to me. Despite this knowledge, I was certain I could learn something more from Declan. It didn't add up that Jason would bail on meetings he had already scheduled for the next day and not mention a word to his friend about it.

"Detective," Declan continues. "I can't help but feel like you are trying to say you suspect I had some involvement in Jason's death."

"I never said anything such, but now that you mention it, is that something I should be looking into?" I inquire, still gauging his reaction.

"Jason was . . . challenging at times. Brilliant, but stubborn." He pauses, looking past me for a moment as if lost in memories. "But I didn't only lose a business partner; I lost a friend. I don't know why he went back to his house. He didn't tell me he was going there, but if I could change the way things happened, I would have."

I make a mental note of his careful phrasing. Intense discussions could mean anything from heated debates to outright arguments. Potential motives lie in what people try to gloss over, in the truths they try to soften with their words.

"Do you have any idea how Jason got down to his house that night?" I ask, more out of curiosity about what his answer will be than actually seeking facts. We already found a car parked down the street from the McAllister residence with plates from the Bay Area. The vehicle was recently processed, and Jason's fingerprints were found inside. It was registered to a business up there. I'm simply waiting on the email from the precinct containing the owner's name so I can call and find out why Jason was in that car that night.

"Detective," he states firmly. "I already told you I didn't even know Jason left the hotel, so how would I know how he got back to LA?"

"One last question," I continue. "I had our tech team try to access the footage from the cameras around the house that night, but the feed seems to end before Mr. McAllister entered the home. Can you tell me how this could happen?"

He looks genuinely puzzled by my question. Without a word, he turns toward his laptop and begins tapping against the keys. Declan suddenly looks even more confused before he clears his throat and says, "It looks like the feed was disabled."

"Disabled?" I repeat. "Can you tell by whom?"

Declan shakes his head. "It was a generic access code. There's no way to know who logged in."

"Who would know how to do that?" I press. "That seems like something only someone at this company would know how to do."

"I don't appreciate you insinuating it could be a member of the Haven family that could be behind this tragic event," he says as I watch his body go rigid. "I don't know who accessed that feed, but I am certain it was no one who works for us."

I jot down a few final notes before snapping the notepad shut, sealing within it the fragments of truth and the layers of evasion that make up this case.

I rise from the leather chair, its surface still warm from my prolonged interrogation. "It seems to me that is something you couldn't possibly be certain of, Mr. Harris. Either way, I appreciate you taking the time to answer my questions. If you think of anything else that might be helpful, please don't hesitate to reach out to me," I say, extending a hand that he shakes with a firmer grip than I expected.

"Of course," he responds, the faintest strain in his smile. "Anything to help get to the bottom of this."

I give him a curt nod and stride toward the door, my steps deliberate. The room feels charged with unsaid thoughts, like static electricity right before a storm. I'm halfway through the threshold when Declan's voice halts me.

"Detective Sanchez," he calls out, and there's something new in his tone—a hint of urgency that wasn't there moments ago.

I turn, an eyebrow raised. "Yes?"

"Before you go," he says, standing now, "I want you to know that everyone here at Haven wants nothing more than to see whoever did this to Jason brought to justice. Would it help to take a look at his office?" His offer hangs between us, a dangling clue I hadn't anticipated. "Maybe there's a chance you'll find something in there that could point you in the right direction."

"That would be very helpful. Thank you," I reply, masking the eagerness that surges through me.

I shadow Declan down the hallway, the soft thud of our steps a counterpoint to the rapid-fire questions ricocheting through my mind.

"Right this way," he murmurs, and there's an undercurrent of something in his voice—nervousness, perhaps, or is it calculation?

We stop before the closed door.

"Here we are," Declan says, glancing at the young lady sitting at the desk outside the door. Her eyes are red and swollen, and she may be the most distraught-looking person I have seen since I caught this case.

"Jenny." Declan clears his throat, and the young girl looks up at him with her glassy stare.

"Yes, Mr. Harris?" Her voice shakes slightly as she speaks.

"This is Detective Sanchez," he continues, and I nod in her direction, offering a tender smile.

"Hello, Detective Sanchez." Jenny's gaze flits nervously between Declan and me, her hands wringing a tissue. It's obvious she's been crying, and I wonder what role she plays in this intricate puzzle surrounding Jason McAllister's death.

"Hi, Jenny, it's nice to meet you," I say, watching as her hand lifts to grip the charm hanging from her necklace.

"Detective Sanchez is here to look through Jason's office," Declan explains to her gently. "Please get her anything she might need."

"Of course," she replies as Declan turns to let me know he is available if I have any other questions before returning to his office.

I smile one last time at Jenny before turning toward Jason's office door. I push the glass door open and walk in. My eyes immediately sweep the room, taking in the meticulously organized shelves of books, the sleek desk, and the large window that overlooks the city below. There's an air of authority in this space, a presence that lingers despite its owner's absence. I immediately notice the difference in tone between Jason's and Declan's offices. You can feel that Jason was a man who wielded power just by standing here.

I pull a pair of latex gloves from my pocket, snapping them against my wrists—a sound punctuating the solemn air. My fingers drift over the desk, pausing over the keyboard, contemplating the emails and messages that might have been sent from here.

I open drawers slowly, methodically, peering inside for anything out of place, any clue Jason might have left behind. My heart beats a steady rhythm, adrenaline mingling with a detective's intuition that every detail could be significant.

I continue my search, eyes scanning, hands feeling for hidden compartments or false bottoms.

Just as I started to lose hope of finding anything substantial, my fingers brushed against something unexpected—a small, leather-bound journal tucked beneath a stack of papers. Curiosity piqued, I carefully extracted the journal and flipped it open to the first page.

The handwriting within is neat and precise. I try to make sense of what I'm reading, and then I see a name. Manhattan AI. Where have I seen that name before? It was familiar, but I didn't know from where. Pulling out my phone, I search for the name, and my stomach drops when I see a news article that features a company staff image from a small start-up. Staring back at me is Lucas's smiling face. What connection did Lucas have with this Manhattan company? Why was Jason so interested in them that he kept detailed notes in this journal hidden at the back of his desk?

After glancing around to ensure no one is watching me, I slide the journal into my messenger bag. My mind races with possibilities.

SIXTEEN

MARIA

Once I finish looking through Jason's office, I step outside and find Jenny sitting quietly. It's obvious that her crying continued while I was inside his office.

"Jenny," I say gently, crouching to her eye level. "Do you need some water or someone to talk to?"

She looks up at me with tear-streaked cheeks, her eyes wide and filled with apprehension. "N-no, I'm okay," she stammers. "I just . . . I just can't believe Jason's gone."

Her voice is fragile, and I can't help but wonder if there is more to her pain than that of an employee grieving her boss.

Jenny takes a deep breath, trying to compose herself. "Detective Sanchez, do you think they'll find out who did this to Jason?" Her voice wavers as she asks the question that weighs heavy on her mind.

"I promise you, Jenny," I reply firmly, meeting her

gaze with determination, "I will do everything in my power to find out the truth and get justice for Jason."

A flicker of hope crosses Jenny's face before it's again clouded by sorrow. "Thank you," she whispers.

"I take it you and your boss were close?"

"Very close." Jenny nods, her eyes cast downward as if wrestling with unspoken thoughts. "He . . . he was like family to me."

After what Declan shared about Jason, I tried to make sense of her statement. "I'm sorry to have to ask this, but I heard Mr. McAllister was difficult to get along with. You seemed so close to him, considering that."

Jenny flashes a half smile and scoffs. "Who said that about him?" she asks but doesn't wait for me to answer. "If anyone didn't get along with Jason, it was only because they didn't understand him. He was the most generous man I had ever met." Her hand tightens around the charm hanging around her neck.

"Did he give you that?" I ask, nodding in the direction of her necklace.

There is a momentary look of guilt in her eyes before she nods.

"Yes, he did," Jenny replies softly, her fingers tracing the charm. "Jason had this way of making you feel like you were the most important person in his life."

Her words linger in the air, and I can't help but wonder about the complexities of Jason McAllister that seem to elude easy characterization.

"Did Mrs. McAllister know . . ." I choose my words carefully. "How close the two of you were?"

She shrugs, and I see a wave of guilt wash over her face, but then quickly disappear. "She was too busy with her own calendar to notice who Jason's friends were."

Jenny's response piques my curiosity. The idea of a close bond between Jason and his employees raises questions, so I decide to probe further. "Did Jason ever confide in you about his personal life, Jenny?" I ask gently, watching her reaction closely.

Jenny hesitates before responding, her eyes flickering with uncertainty. "He . . . he did," she admits hesitantly, her voice barely above a whisper. "He had concerns about . . . about his wife, Victoria." A pang of sympathy crosses her face before she quickly composes herself.

"Concerns?" I prompt, leaning in slightly as if urging her to share more.

She takes a deep breath, steeling herself before continuing. "He was worried she might be having an affair," Jenny reveals, her words hanging heavy in the air between us.

"He told you that?" I inquire.

"Well, no . . ."

"Then what makes you say that?"

She hesitates before pulling open her desk drawer to reveal a folder. Looking up at me wide-eyed, she says, "I'm sorry. I don't know why I took it."

I reach in and pull the folder out, flipping through

the images of Victoria with Lucas. None were precisely damning, but there were a couple where they definitely looked like more than teacher and student.

"Jason has me pay Marshall off the books, so when I found out what happened to him, I thought maybe the work Marshall did had something to do with it, so I went and looked in Jason's office for the file Marshall brought him the other day." Jenny's words are spilling from her mouth at high speed.

"Slow down," I say, closing the folder and dropping it into my messenger bag. "Who's Marshall?"

"He's the . . ." She looks around to make sure nobody is listening before she whispers, "You know, the fixer."

"Fixer?" I question as I shake my head.

She nods. "Yeah. If someone has a problem, call Marshall, and he fixes it."

I tilt my head curiously as I consider if Jason had gone and gotten himself fixed somehow by this Marshall character. "Do you have this Marshall's contact info?"

"I'm not supposed to," Jenny replies before she nervously bites at her top lip. "But he slipped me his business card last time he was here and said we should go grab a drink sometime."

"Do you have that?"

She nods and grabs her purse, digging inside for a moment before retrieving it and handing me a card.

The card is simple, with only a name and number. I

slip it into my pocket, making a mental note to investigate this fixer named Marshall.

"Thank you, Jenny," I say as I stand. "You've been accommodating."

As I turn to leave, Jenny hesitates before calling after me, "Detective Sanchez . . . I'm not a bad person and neither was Jason."

"My job isn't to decide who is good and bad. My job is to find out who did this to Jason," I say with a forced smile as I turn and walk away. I've met women like Jenny before. They are fed some ridiculous story about the terrible wife at home who doesn't love them and doesn't understand them. They are so eager to be loved they never stop questioning whether the story they are being told is just that. A story.

The last woman I caught my husband cheating with told me about all the lies he had told her about me. She thought it would somehow make me feel better to know that she hadn't slept with my husband, knowing that I wasn't anything like what he had portrayed. What none of these women seem to understand is that they are the ones who chose to sleep with married men. I had nothing to do with it, just as Victoria had nothing to do with Jenny's choice to sleep with Jason. It's not our job to justify their choices or absolve them of their sins.

I make my way back to my car, the weight of the case heavy on my shoulders. My thoughts are wrapped up in this new character, Marshall. What did Jason McAllister need a fixer for? What else had he used this man for? Had Marshall assisted in fixing something for Jason when it came to the Manhattan AI company? Or more than that, how many people could want revenge for the things Jason used this man to do?

My phone begins to ring, interrupting my thoughts. I'm surprised when I answer and hear Victoria McAllister's voice on the other end.

"Detective Sanchez?" Victoria's voice is shaky.

"Mrs. McAllister, I was beginning to wonder if I was going to hear from you," I reply, noting the tremor in her tone.

"I'm sorry . . . it's just been so hard."

"I understand, but you have to understand I have a lot of questions I need to ask you about your husband," I push back.

"Of course." Victoria's voice is barely above a whisper, filled with a mix of fear and desperation. "I know this is a lot to ask, but the press has been parked outside the hotel since I arrived. Is there any way that you can come by here?"

I agree, and she rattles off the information I need to go to her.

After hanging up the phone with Victoria, I dial Bishop to let him know about all the new information, but it goes straight to voicemail. I hang up and try again with the same result. If Bishop is going to be checked out on this case as much as he was on our other ones, I decide I might as well put him to work on something tight that might prove useful.

This time, when I get Bishop's voicemail, I leave him

a detailed message instructing him to follow up on the location of Jason's cell phone, the registration in the car Jason was driving that night, and to check on the lab work that the chief had put a rush on. I can't help but smirk when I hang up, knowing how annoyed he will be with me telling him what to do. It's probably my happiest moment in months.

SEVENTEEN

MARIA

I tap the steering wheel, my gaze fixed on the multiple press vans gathered near the hotel entrance. My phone lies in the passenger seat. I know Victoria is waiting for me, but I can't shake the feeling that the first interaction I need to have is with this so-called fixer.

With a steadying breath, I snatch up the phone and type in the number sweet Jenny supplied me with. My pulse dances in my wrists as I press Call.

"Hello?" A voice breaks through the ringing.

"Hello. This is Detective Sanchez speaking," I say. "I believe you have recently done some work for a client that warrants a discussion."

"I'm not sure who you mean, Detective," he says, his voice smooth like polished stone.

"Did you recently do some work for Jason McAllister?" I continue.

"Yes, ma'am," he replies. "Is everything okay?"

His words are careful and deliberate, and I wonder

if he genuinely hasn't heard about his client's dire fate. "I'm investigating a murder, and your name has surfaced in conjunction with some . . . sensitive details."

"I can assure you that I had nothing to do with any murder," he replies, his tone nonchalant, almost bored. "Mr. McAllister contracts me to take care of things for him, but always within the confines of the law."

His answer sounds rehearsed, and my back stiffens in annoyance. Men like him practically flaunt the fact that they happily break the law for the wealthy of LA.

"Interesting," I say, my voice cool and collected. "I'm not sure why I would ever think Mr. McAllister contracted you to kill himself."

"Wait—what?" His surprise registers as genuine. "Jason's dead?"

"He is. Do you happen to know if Mr. McAllister had any enemies who would have wanted him dead? Or perhaps you had any beef with your other client, Manhattan AI?"

"I facilitate needs. I help reveal secrets, and I make problems disappear. That's it."

The nonchalance in his voice sends shivers down my spine. "Including murder?" I question sharply.

A chuckle on the other end of the line is low and dangerous. "I never said that, Detective. But rest assured, I only take work within the confines of the law."

I take a moment to digest his words before asking, "Let me ask you again. Do you have any idea who might have wanted Jason McAllister dead?"

"Can't say that I do," he replies easily. "Jason hired me to follow his wife, and I did as he asked—that's it. I do know one thing. Whatever happened to Jason that night wasn't part of the plan."

"Part of what plan?" I press.

The man hesitates before admitting, "Jason had asked if I could help him source some Rohypnol."

"For what?"

"I don't ask those types of questions from my client's, Detective."

"But you always work within the confines of the law, huh?" I huff.

"I do, but I can't help what my clients choose to do."

"And did you help him?"

"I believe he did obtain some," he confirms before backpedaling, "but of course, I can't be certain."

"Uh-huh," I continue with an involuntary eye roll. "What do you know about Jason's dealings with Manhattan AI?"

"Manhattan AI?" His voice is smooth. "Jason approached me for a job some time ago." There's a pause. "But I had to decline. Conflicting interests with existing clients. You understand how these things work."

I scribble on my notepad, his words dancing between lines of possible meanings. The refusal speaks volumes; it screams loyalty or fear, maybe both.

"I see." I clear my throat before I continue. "I saw the pictures you provided Mr. McAllister of his wife."

"I feel uncomfortable discussing my client's private matters, Detective."

"Yeah, well, your client is dead, so you may want to get uncomfortable before I consider you a suspect," I warn.

Marshall scoffs at my suggestion. "I'm in Mexico on client work, so you can look into me all you want. I'm confident you won't find anything because I didn't do anything."

I sigh, making a mental note to look into Marshall's alibi. "Can you confirm if you ever witnessed Mrs. McAllister actually engaged in . . . well, in an affair? The pictures I saw only confirm a single kiss."

"No, Detective. I never saw them actually engage in any physical acts of intimacy," Marshall replies smoothly, his words leaving a trail of doubt in its wake. "But I tend to find where there is smoke, there's fire."

I jot down his response, feeling the weight of his words as they linger in the air. "Right." I pause, trying to read between the lines of Marshall's composed demeanor. "Do you have any knowledge of why Jason McAllister was in Los Angeles that night when he was supposed to be in San Francisco?"

There's a brief silence on the other end of the line before Marshall finally speaks. "I'm afraid I don't, Detective. My interactions with Mr. McAllister were strictly professional."

A flicker of suspicion darts through me. Marshall's responses feel carefully crafted to conceal his client's secrets. "Well, Mr. Marshall, I appreciate your cooperation. We may need to speak further upon your return from Mexico."

"Of course, Detective," Marshall replies smoothly. "I'll make myself available for any further questions you may have."

As the call ends, I sit back in my seat, mulling over the conversation. Lucas and Victoria both complained about feeling incredibly tired, then waking up with a headache before discovering Mr. McAllister's body. The Rohypnol Jason requested from his fixer explains that, but to what end? He wouldn't have knocked out his wife and the man he believed to be her lover only to shoot himself. It doesn't make sense.

Did Jason have more sinister plans when he approached his home that night? Was there someone lying in wait for him? Someone who knew they could turn the tables on Mr. McAllister?

EIGHTEEN

MARIA

The lower level of the parking garage is dim. The flickering fluorescent lights cast long shadows between the rows of cars. Taking a deep breath, I exit my vehicle and head toward the stairwell. Reaching the door marked with peeling gold numbers, I pause, slipping my badge inside my shirt to conceal it. Based on the amount of press I saw parked in front of Victoria's hotel, the last thing I want to do is have someone notice an officer heading up to her room. This entire experience must be hard enough on her as it is.

I still haven't decided whether I believe Victoria and Lucas's version of their relationship and that it never went beyond friendship. Still, even if she's lying about that, something tells me she's telling the truth when she says she did not kill her husband. From what I can gather, Jason McAllister did not seem to be a well-liked man, and it's clear he didn't trust anyone around him, based on the company he kept.

I slip inside the hotel's back entrance and am relieved when I don't see anyone as I approach the elevator. I step inside and press the number to the floor Victoria had relayed on the phone.

The elevator doors slide open with a soft ding. I step out onto a plush carpeted hallway lined with elegant wallpaper and soft lighting. Walking to Victoria's room, I raise my hand to knock on the door.

After a moment, the door creaks open, revealing Victoria standing there, her eyes slightly puffy from crying. She offers me a small smile before stepping back to let me in. The room is neat and orderly, a contrast to her disheveled appearance. She ushers me inside with a handful of apologies. The hotel room is an elegant suite, and she takes a seat on the sofa near the drawn curtains. I sit opposite her as she nervously wrings her hands in her lap. Clearing my throat, I begin to speak.

"Victoria, I know this must be difficult for you, but I need to ask you more questions. Can you walk me through the events of that evening one more time?"

She nods slowly and starts recounting the events leading up to Jason's death. Her story hasn't changed since we first spoke, and it matches Lucas's version of the evening. Her voice wavers at times, and I can see the pain etched in every line of her face.

As she finishes speaking, I reach into my pocket and pull out the envelope with photos Jason hired Marshall to take of his wife. Placing them on the table between us, I watch Victoria's eyes widen in shock. She picks them up and quickly flips through them, her mouth falling open.

"Where did you get these?" she asks, unable to avert her eyes from the images.

"We found these pictures of you in Jason's office. Do you have any idea why he would have someone following you?"

Victoria's gaze lingers a moment longer on the photos before meeting mine with a steely determination.

"I knew someone was following me," Victoria admits, her voice more robust now, her eyes narrowing in resolve. "I didn't know Jason had hired them."

"Who else would want to follow you, Mrs. McAllister?"

She scoffs, "This isn't the first time I have caught someone taking pictures of me, Detective. My husband moves in circles of very powerful men, and some of them would love to find anything juicy they think would be useful to blackmail Jason into doing what they want."

"So you knew you were being followed?"

She nods in response. "I saw someone taking pictures of me, but I don't think he knew I saw him." She pulled out the picture of her kissing Lucas and slid it across the coffee table to me. "That's why I kissed Lucas. Not because I'm having an affair with him but because I thought I would mess with whoever thought it was okay to follow me around and invade my privacy like that."

"Weren't you afraid whoever was taking the pictures would take that image back to your husband?"

Victoria sighs. "Honestly, I wasn't thinking straight. I thought I would make the idiot behind it all look like a fool when they tried to blackmail us for an affair that I wasn't even having. It was such an impulsive and stupid thing to do. I had no idea it was Jason who was having me followed."

She hesitates, and her face contorts into one of horror as her eyes go glassy.

"What is it?" I ask as I look around the room for a box of tissues. I retrieve them and hand her the box before sitting again.

"Do you think Jason thought I was—that Lucas and me—" Her words drop off as she pulls out a tissue and lifts it to her mouth.

"That's exactly what I think your husband thought," I confirm without making her say the words. "And I think he came back to your home that night with the intention of hurting you and possibly Lucas as well." She avoids looking at me, her eyes fixed on the pile of pictures splayed out on the coffee table. "If Jason came there that night and attacked the two of you, I believe a jury would see that as self-defense, but you have to come clean with me, Mrs. McAllister, sooner than later."

Her eyes dart up to me, and she forgets about the tears streaming down her cheeks momentarily. Clearing her throat, she looks pointedly at me. "I did not kill my husband."

"Did Lucas?"

Victoria hesitates for a moment. Finally, she shakes her head. "I told you before. I drank the champagne, and the next thing I knew, I woke up and found Jason dead. I don't remember anything else."

I study her carefully, trying to read between the lines. "You didn't really answer my question. What about Lucas? Do you think he could have done this?"

Victoria sits upright and grips the tissue in her fist, clearly growing frustrated with my questions. "No, no way. Lucas would have no reason to hurt Jason," she insists, though there's a hint of uncertainty in her voice.

"You don't seem sure."

She huffs. "I'm not saying Lucas did this because I'm certain he didn't."

"But?"

"But . . . I did think it was weird how adamant he was that Jason not find out I was helping him with the real estate stuff. When I asked him why, all he said was Jason would be upset if he found out he was leaving the company because of how he got the job in the first place."

"How did he get the job?" I press, sensing we might be getting closer to the truth.

"Lucas never told me," Victoria replies with a shrug. "But knowing Jason, it was probably something underhanded."

I take in Victoria's words, mulling over the new information she's provided. Every thread I pull seems to lead to a darker revelation surrounding Jason McAllister.

"Victoria . . ." I wonder if asking the question is wise or will cause her to shut down. "Did you love your husband?" I eventually ask, watching for her reaction.

To my surprise, Victoria doesn't flinch at the blunt question. Instead, she meets my gaze head-on, her expression resolute.

"He was an asshole," she admits, her voice laced with bitterness. "But that doesn't mean I didn't love him in some twisted way. Jason was the type of man who could have had anyone he wanted. He exuded confidence and power, and he chose me. I know it sounds awful, but as shitty as things were sometimes, I always held that. He chose me out of all the women he could have been with."

I nod in understanding, knowing all too well the complexities of human emotions. Sometimes love and hate can exist side by side, intertwined in a tangled mess we can't even unravel.

"Can I ask when was the last time you heard from Jason that night?" I circle back around, hoping for a new sliver of evidence to point me in a new direction.

Victoria's gaze drifts past me, settling somewhere in the middle distance as she begins to recount the evening. "Jason phoned around eight," she starts, her voice measured but tinged with a note of distress. "He said the conference welcome events would probably go late into the night."

"If he called you at eight, he must have already been on the road at that time. If I had to guess, he was trying to figure out when you would be home," I say as I think aloud.

"None of this makes sense," she cries, and I can see her hands starting to tremble. "Jason would never hurt me."

I study Victoria's expression, the furrow of her brow, and the way her fingers twist nervously in her lap. "I'm sorry to be the one to tell you this, but your husband wasn't only having you followed. He also acquired some Rohypnol right before his trip." She blinks at me repeatedly as if having trouble processing my words. "Didn't you say that he purchased a bottle of your favorite champagne for you? Is that something out of character for him?"

Victoria's eyes widen in shock at my revelation. She sits there, frozen momentarily before the puzzle pieces click into place in her mind. Her hand flies to her mouth, muffling a gasp as she processes the implications of what I've just disclosed. "He . . . he roofied me?" Victoria whispers, her voice barely above a breath. The disbelief is palpable in how her body tenses, her entire frame recoiling at the thought of such betrayal from her husband.

"It seems that way," I confirm gently.

"That fucking piece of shit." Her quiet and fragile demeanor has slipped away and been replaced with a fierce rage. "He fucking knew what he was up to. That fucking piece of shit."

I shake my head in confusion. "Who knew what who was up to?"

"Declan. That bastard must have known what Jason was planning to do," she answers, and I can see her mind spinning.

"Your husband's business partner?" I inquire. "What makes you say that?"

"Declan called me about a week ago, which I thought was strange because we don't really talk much these days," she says. "He suggested I might not want to be spending so much time with company employees. I thought maybe whoever was having me followed told Declan or something, but when I asked him about it, all he would say was that I should be careful. Oh, and that Lucas might not be as innocent as he seems."

"What do you think he meant by that?"

"I asked him!" she exclaims. "He said some bullshit about how Lucas has a certain reputation for being . . . ambitious. For doing whatever is necessary to climb the ladder."

"And what did you make of that?" I ask, probing gently.

She shrugs, almost dismissively. "I didn't know what to think. I asked Declan if Jason had put him up to it, and he said as far as he knew, Jason was unaware of my friendship with Lucas and that it would be better for me if it stayed that way. But come on, clearly, reaching out to me was just a way to clear his conscience."

"How so?"

"If Jason was really willing to drug me, make sure he had an alibi, and then drive down here and kill me, I would bet money he discussed his plan with his shit-head of a business partner. It makes total sense why he called me now." She shakes her head wildly and crosses her arms over her chest. "Jesus, I can't believe I actually thought he was trying to do me a favor."

I take in Victoria's words, the newfound anger and betrayal simmering beneath the surface. Declan's sudden warning and cryptic insinuations only add another layer of complexity to the already convoluted case. As I watch Victoria, her eyes burning with a mix of emotions, I can't help but feel a surge of determination to get to the bottom of this twisted web of lies.

"I need you to think carefully," I say. "Did Jason ever say anything that would make you suspicious of Declan? Anything that might indicate Declan may have been involved in what your husband may have been planning?"

Her gaze flickers, her mind racing as she sifts through her memories. After a moment, she shakes her head slowly. "No, I told you everything that was discussed," she replies, her tone heavy with contemplation.

I nod thoughtfully. "We are still looking into all leads, but if Declan reaches out to you, I need you to avoid his calls. Do you understand me? At least until we know a little more."

Victoria's expression hardens with resolve as she meets my eyes. "You don't think Declan may want to hurt me, do you?"

I shake my head. "We haven't seen any indication of

that, but this investigation still has a lot of moving pieces, and I want to be cautious. Okay?"

Victoria's jaw sets in a determined line as she nods in agreement. "Okay, I'll do what you say. I just want to know the truth about what happened that night."

With a reassuring smile, I rise from my seat and offer Victoria a nod of acknowledgment. "We'll get to the bottom of this, Victoria. I promise you that."

This case is far from over, and with each new revelation, it seems to only grow more twisted and intricate. As I make my way out of Victoria's hotel room, one thing is clear—there is more to Jason's death than meets the eye.

NINETEEN

MARIA

As I slide into the driver's seat, a buzz from my pocket pulls me out of my thoughts. My phone lights up with Bishop's name dancing across the screen. I let out a sigh before answering, knowing what was coming.

"Sanchez," I answer in a clipped tone, readying myself for the inevitable.

"Look, Maria," Bishop says, and I can hear the frustration in his voice. "I don't really appreciate you having me running around like some errand boy. Next time you think about bossing me around, it would serve you well to remember I'm your partner and not your assistant."

I grip the steering wheel tighter, feeling heat rise to my cheeks, not from anger but from the effort it takes to remain calm. "Of course, you're not my assistant, but how many times do we have to do this dance?" I try to keep my voice level. "Every time I question a witness, I give you the option to come along. But you always have something else on your plate."

"Oh, pardon me if I don't always make myself readily available at your beck and call, Princess," he snarls.

As much as every single muscle in my body wants to tell him off, I know it will only result in a complaint to HR. Taking a deep breath, I exhale slowly and find my Zen before I do my best to reframe Bishop's point of view. "You're right," I say, stalling my pride. "You're my partner, and I should have explained that I needed someone with experience to follow up on those leads."

"What are you talking about?" he grumbles, his curiosity piqued.

"I have a feeling those 'errands,' as you call them, are crucial pieces to this case. They might be exactly what we need to break it wide open. I thought your experience might shed some light where I couldn't."

There's a brief pause on the other end of the line, and I can practically hear Bishop processing my words. Finally, he lets out a slow exhale that almost sounds like defeat. "Fine, fine, Maria. I get it." It's almost too easy, but I've learned to play the game if it gets us through another day without butting heads.

"Besides," I add, starting the ignition and glancing at the rearview mirror, "you're good at what you do. The best, even. We all have our roles to play, and right now, I need you working your magic to make sure none of the evidence falls through the cracks."

I pull out onto the street, leaving Victoria's hotel behind. I await Bishop's response, hoping my words have smoothed his ruffled feathers.

"Alright, alright, that's enough of that," Bishop grumbles. "I have something for you. Jason's phone—the one we've been waiting on—it's turned up."

"It has?"

"Yup, the tech team has it now. They're working their magic to unlock it."

"That's amazing, good work." I wince as I congratulate him for doing the most basic aspect of his job.

"Oh, and you know the car with McAllister's fingerprints? The one he used that night?"

I want to shout in response that, of course, I know the car he's talking about because I told him to finish the trace on the vehicle. I bite back my harsh response and soften my tone as I respond, "Yeah, what about it?"

"I did some digging. Called up the owner. Turns out Jason borrowed the car last minute and told the guy it was urgent."

"Urgent?"

"Yep. And here's the kicker—he made the owner swear to keep quiet about it." Bishop continues. "The owner is some business acquaintance from years back. Says Jason did him a solid once, so he didn't ask questions. He had no clue Jason would head back to LA with the car. He didn't even know he had left San Francisco. Apparently, he expected Jason to return the car before he left town."

"Do you believe him?" I press, eyes narrowing at the open road ahead.

"Seemed to be on the level. Shocked as hell when I told him where we found his car."

"Good work, Bishop." The praise comes easier this time.

"Thought you'd like that," he replies, a note of self-satisfaction threading his words.

I glance at the clock on the dashboard; its digits are a stark reminder that I'm running late. I'm not in the mood for the guilt trip that comes along with picking my teen up late this evening.

"Okay, I need to wrap this up, Bishop. I'm heading to pick up my kid."

"Kids," he grunts, and I can hear the disdain in that one word as if it's a concept so foreign to him it might as well be extraterrestrial. "Glad I never got tied down by any rugrats."

I bite back the retort clawing up my throat. I dream of the day Bishop hands in his badge—a day when I no longer have to tolerate his lazy, chauvinistic ass. For now, I grit my teeth and do my best to ignore his countless annoying personality flaws.

"Anyway," I continue, "I'll type up the notes from Victoria's interview and send them to you tonight."

"Make sure you do," he says, the line crackling with the underlying demand for efficiency.

"Always do." I keep my tone even and professional.

I end the call with Bishop, feeling a mix of relief and

frustration. His arrogance always manages to get under my skin. There isn't much else I can do tonight, but something tells me Jason's phone might hold some answers we've been searching for.

TWENTY

MARIA

The photos of Victoria and Lucas are sprawled out across my coffee table. I study them as I take a sip of wine. My eyes flicker from photo to photo, seeking anything I may have missed. The living room is silent, save for the buzzing of the refrigerator on its last leg in the kitchen.

Suddenly, a sound from the hallway startles me. I glance up to see my daughter, Jordan. The first thing I notice is her eyes filled with guilt and defiance.

I raise an eyebrow, silently urging her to speak.

"M-Mom. I . . . I have something to tell you," Jordan says, biting her lip nervously. She hesitates before blurting out, "I've been skipping school."

My heart sinks as anger and disappointment rise inside me. Before I can even respond, Jordan continues in a rush: "The principal called me into his office today and told me he's going to suspend me."

I struggle to process what she's saying. "Wait." I

shake my head. “I don’t understand. You’ve been skipping school? Why would you do such a thing?” My mind is a jumbled mess of thoughts, and I’m left wondering how things could have spiraled to this point without me noticing. Clearly, I am not the detective I thought I was.

“It’s not that big a deal, okay? So don’t freak out.”

“Not that big a deal!” I exclaim, my face flushing hot in frustration. “You’ve been skipping school to the point where you got yourself suspended. That’s a huge deal, Mijo.”

“Don’t call me that. God, you sound just like Grandma when you say it,” she huffs, and I can’t understand why she doesn’t seem to be focusing on the actual problem in front of us.

“You didn’t answer me,” I press. “If you haven’t been at school, then where have you been?” She crosses her arms and looks away from me defiantly.

She flinches as if the question is a slap, her eyes darting to the floor. “Around,” she mumbles, but it’s not an answer. Not even close.

“Around isn’t a place!” My voice spikes with frustration, the detective in me wrestling with the mother, both equally fierce and equally scared. “Is it some boy? Tell me it’s not some boy.” The last thing I need is history repeating itself with my daughter.

Jordan’s head snaps up, her eyes flashing with anger that matches my own. “So what if it is? You’d know all about that, wouldn’t you?” Her words are barbed.

I’m taken aback. My hands are trembling now; I

clench them into fists. "I just don't want you to make the same mistakes I did."

"Oh, so that's how you see me—a mistake?" Her voice cracks, but the defiance in her eyes doesn't waver.

"Dammit, you're not—you've never been a mistake. You know what I meant." The room feels like it's closing in on me. "I made mistakes, yes, but you're the one thing I got right." My voice softens, pleading with her to understand. "You're my everything. I can't stand the thought of you throwing away your future."

She looks at me then, really looks at me, and I can see the turmoil behind her gaze. I hold my breath, waiting for her to let me in. But the silence stretches between us.

"Please tell me, where were you?" I plead.

She hesitates, shifting her weight from foot to foot as if preparing to run or fight. It's a stance I recognize all too well, which fractures something inside me. "Why can't you trust me? Why do you always assume the worst?"

"Because I'm your mom. Because I care," I rattle off all the reasons. "Hell, how about because I love you more than anyone."

Finally, she breaks, her shoulders slumping as if unloading an unbearable weight. "Dad." The name falls flat, an unwelcome guest in our home.

"What about him?" My voice is barely a whisper, a tremor betraying the walls I've built.

Jordan looks down at her shoes, avoiding my gaze. "I-I've been going to see Dad," she admits quietly.

The mention of her father hits me like a punch to the gut. Memories flood back—the betrayal, the lies. Jordan saw how he ripped this family apart with his selfishness. The fact that she's been sneaking off to visit him behind my back leaves me speechless.

"I don't understand. You can see your father whenever you want. Why would you skip school to see him? Did he know you were skipping? He approved of it? I'm going to kill—"

"Mom! Stop!" Jordan shouts. "He didn't know. I told him I was on break."

"On break?" I scoff. "He should have known that was a lie. How did you even get there?"

"I took a bus," she huffs. "I told Dad you were dropping me off and picking me up, but instead, I was taking a bus."

"Jordan, you know I don't like you taking a bus to that area alone. How could you be so stupid?"

"Because I miss him, okay?" Her voice cracks, and suddenly, I wish I hadn't been so harsh with my words. "I get that you don't love him anymore, but he's still my dad."

"I would never keep you from seeing him," I insist. "All you have to do is ask."

"I do ask! All the time. You're always too busy with work to take me to see him." Her words bite at me, and I have no defense. She's right. I've repeatedly told her it's not a convenient time. Before I can agree with her, Jordan whirls around a storm of teenage defiance and storms off, slamming her bedroom door behind her.

The silence that follows is oppressive, a suffocating blanket of self-doubt. I sink into the chair. I have always tried to live a life dedicated to justice and to protect others. But who protects my daughter from the fallout of my choices? How can I focus on helping strangers when my own anger has blinded me to the pain I am putting my daughter through?

Pushing myself up out of my chair, I make my way down the dimly lit hall to my daughter's bedroom. The pictures on the walls stare back at me—snapshots of happier times, mocking me with their frozen smiles.

Taking a deep breath, I knock on Jordan's door and gently push it open. She sits on her bed, her back to me, tension radiating from her still form.

"Jordan," I say, my voice softer now, stripped of the earlier sharpness. "I'm sorry."

She doesn't turn, but I see her shoulders relax ever so slightly.

"I shouldn't have reacted that way. I let my frustration with . . . everything else get the better of me." I tentatively step into her room, giving her space yet closing the emotional distance between us. "But we need to talk about why you're skipping school. We can find a way for you to spend time with your father without compromising your education."

Her silence weighs heavily between us, a barrier built of stubbornness and hurt. I know this won't be easy.

"Your education is important. It's your future. And I won't stand by and watch you jeopardize it."

She turns, her eyes searching mine for the assurance this isn't another empty promise. "You mean it?"

"Absolutely." I move closer before perching on the edge of her bed. "We'll figure it out. But please, no more skipping school, okay?"

"Okay," she whispers. Something shifts between us. I reach out, and this time, she doesn't pull away. My arms encircle her.

"Listen to me," I say with a newfound steadiness. "I've been letting the job take over, and that's on me. But I'm going to change that. You're my priority."

She bites her lip before saying, "I just want things to be normal, Mom. Like they used to be."

Jordan leans into me again, her body language shedding the armor of her teenage rebellion. It's as if she's permitting herself to be my little girl for a moment longer before the rush of adolescence sweeps her away once more. We sit in silence until she finds the courage to add, "You know, not every man is like Dad. There are guys out there who'd treat you right."

Her words catch me off guard, a reminder that even as I've been trying to protect her from my heartaches, she's been watching, learning, and forming her own opinions. I let out a soft chuckle, ruffling her hair affectionately. "Let me worry about my love life, kiddo. Your job is to be a kid and focus on school and friends. Well, that and trying not to give your old mom too many gray hairs."

She grins, the tension easing from her features.

"Okay, but just so you know, you deserve someone amazing."

"Thank you, sweetheart. That means a lot." The simplicity of her faith in me warms my heart. She nods, her eyes bright.

"Now, let's get some sleep. It's been a long day for both of us."

As Jordan settles under the covers, I linger at the doorway, watching her drift toward sleep. Her earlier words echo in my mind. Maybe someone out there can offer the love and respect I've always wanted.

The house is silent now, and as I make my way to my own bed, my thoughts shift to Jason McAllister. Clearly, Jason wasn't a good man and certainly not a good husband. Could someone have seen the way he treated Victoria? Was his life snuffed out—possibly by someone who fancied themselves a savior or maybe a rival? Lucas's name surfaces in my mind. Could Lucas have become so smitten with Victoria without her realizing it?

Victoria had mentioned something . . . Yes, Declan. He had called her, warning her to keep her distance from Lucas. Jealousy can drive a person to extremes, and if Declan believed Jason's version of events, he must have thought Victoria was having an affair with Lucas. What if his warning to Victoria was motivated by his own feelings for Victoria? Perhaps he saw Jason's plotting as the perfect chance to set a trap for him and pin it all on young Lucas.

My pulse quickens at the thought, my instincts as a

detective flaring to life. Declan was supposed to be in San Francisco at the time of Jason's murder. However, Jason managed to make it down to LA. Maybe Declan could have followed.

It's a long shot, but everything about this case has been murky and convoluted from the start. Sleep eludes me as I settle into bed, my mind racing with possibilities and suspicions. For now, the case will have to wait. Sleep is beckoning me.

TWENTY-ONE

MARIA

When I step into the precinct, I'm greeted by the familiar scent of stale coffee and printer toner. The room is buzzing, more alive at this time of day than when I usually arrive. After a few more steps toward my desk, I jump, startled by my partner's booming voice.

"Sanchez!" he calls across the room. With his trademark smirk, Bishop leans against the frame of his office door. "I was about to put out a missing person alert for you. Never thought I'd see the day the sunrise would beat you getting here."

I chuckle, dropping my bag near my desk without breaking my stride toward him. "Bishop, normally, if you managed to show up before me, we'd have to declare it a national holiday. However, I made an exception today and decided to come in a little later."

"An exception? Oh lord, now I know you must have hit your head or something. You are the biggest creature of habit if I've ever seen one," he scoffs. "What in the world would have you making an exception?"

"My daughter, if you must know," I reply, catching a momentary glimpse of his eye roll. She needed some mother-daughter quality time, so I took her to breakfast."

He takes a seat at his desk chair and then crosses his arms over his puffed-out chest. "I see. Well, while you were off bonding," he says the word with such disdain that it feels dirty somehow, "I was here working when they dropped off McAllister's autopsy and labs."

I raise an eyebrow in surprise. "Wait, really? Already?"

"Yeah, must be nice to be buddies with the mayor," Bishop grunts.

Confused, I shake my head. "What does it matter if being buddies gets you this speediness when you are dead and can't enjoy it?"

He shrugs. "True."

"So? What did they find?" I ask impatiently after a few moments of silence settles between us.

Bishop grabs the files off his desk and hands them to me. "Gunshot wound was the cause of death, no surprises there. However, there was definitely blunt force trauma to the back of the head. They were unable to match what could have caused the wound. But, get this—the only fingerprints on the gun belonged to Mr. McAllister."

My mind starts racing as I flip through the documents. "This doesn't make any sense," I say as I read a puzzling line on the autopsy report.

"What doesn't?"

"The section about if it was homicide or self-inflicted says inconclusive," I reply. "He had a wound to the back of the head, so clearly someone attacked him. He lies about where he is going to be, drives to LA, has a gun on him, and then what . . . shoots himself?"

"I don't think the doc is saying it's suicide, more that he can't rule it out," Bishop replies.

"Well, I can," I snap. "Jason McAllister was murdered. There's no doubt in my mind about that."

"Well, there's more," Bishop continues. "There was Rohypnol in the champagne."

I nod. "During my interview with Victoria, she mentioned he brought home her favorite champagne before he left."

Bishop's eyes widen. "Fuck, what was this guy planning?"

"Well, he suspected her of cheating," I add. "Maybe rather than go through a messy divorce, he thought it would be easier to kill her."

"The lab came back with the toxicology reports," Bishop adds, pulling a sheet off the top of the stack on his desk. He hands it over, his expression tight.

I scan the document, absorbing the stark black print against the white paper. The numbers are cold and clinical, but they scream their silent story at me. "Both of them had Rohypnol in their systems," I read aloud, "but Victoria . . . she had more. Much more. How does that work?"

Bishop shrugs. "Maybe she drank more, or perhaps it's the size difference between the two."

"Hmm . . . maybe," I mutter, deep in thought.

I shake my head slowly, dispelling the lingering fog of assumptions. "Bishop," I start, fixing my gaze on him as I straighten from leaning against the cool metal of my desk. "We've been playing with the idea that Victoria and Lucas were more than friends—because it's easy and fits a narrative we're used to. But they both swore up and down they were just platonic."

"People lie, especially when they've got something to hide." Bishop retorts skepticism etched into the lines of his forehead.

"True," I concede. "But maybe we're looking at this all wrong. Maybe we need to stop searching for smoke where there's no fire."

Bishop rubs at his jaw, the stubble there whispering protest under his fingers. He looks unconvinced but curious. "So why drug them both?" he asks, eyes narrowing in thought.

"Because . . ." I let the theory settle into my bones before I voice it. "Jason wasn't aiming for Lucas. He went there with one goal in mind: to kill his wife." The words hang heavy between us, charged with the gravity of premeditated murder.

"Kill Victoria?" Bishop's voice rises, incredulous. "But why? Why go through all this trouble of killing the wife and plan to leave Lucas alive?"

"Because," I say. "One, Jason McAllister doesn't strike me as the kind of man who accepts losing. And two, I think he planned to pin the murder on Lucas all along. He wanted revenge on both of them. What better way to throw suspicion off yourself than to put it on someone else? He knocks them out, kills his wife, and stages the scene. Then he drives back up to San Francisco before Lucas even wakes up."

"Okay, so what went wrong?" Bishop asks, and I wish I knew the answer. "I mean, don't get me wrong, I like your theory. Jealousy's a hell of a motive, but if Jason planned to kill her, how do you explain him being the one in the morgue?"

I shuffle the stack of photographs on my desk, each one a frozen moment of the McAllister crime scene.

"That's a good question." I exhale, glancing over at Bishop, and state, "That's why we need to talk to Lucas Flynn again. Victoria told me that whatever Lucas did to get his position at Haven wasn't something he wanted to tell her about. I have a feeling that boy knows more than he's telling us."

"Okay," Bishop says, standing and grabbing his blazer off the back of the chair. "But you drive. I got in here so early I need a nap on the way."

"You're going with me?" I ask him, not bothering to shield my surprise.

"Better than sitting around here waiting for you to give me a chore list," he grumbles as he walks past me toward the parking lot. I take off in a sprint to catch up with him.

TWENTY-TWO

MARIA

Bishop takes the lead as we exit the elevator onto the floor of the Haven offices. The receptionist eyes us with a practiced smile. Bishop flashes his badge and explains we are here to see Lucas. She furrows her brow with a confused look.

"Lucas?" She repeats the name.

"Lucas Flynn," I reply, watching as she glances over the directory. She picks up the phone a moment later, murmuring something we can't quite catch, then gestures for us to wait in a nearby conference room.

Minutes tick by. I watch Bishop drum his fingers on the table, his jaw clenched in anticipation. Finally, the door creaks open, and Lucas walks in, nervous energy radiating from him. He closes the door behind him and sits at the table opposite us.

"I can't believe you showed up at work," Lucas mutters, looking around through the glass walls to see if anyone is watching the meeting. "Why are you here?"

"We're here to get answers you didn't seem to think we needed the first time around," Bishop snaps, and it becomes clear once again why I hate doing interviews with this man.

"I told you everything I know," Lucas insists.

I place a hand on Bishop's arm to indicate to him that I think it would be best if I take the lead. "I'm sorry that we had to come here to talk with you, but we felt like this was something that couldn't wait."

"What was?" His response is strained.

"I spoke with Victoria McAllister yesterday, and she mentioned that she believes you were brought onto Haven AI under nefarious circumstances," I say. His eyes widen in shock. "We were hoping you could shed some light on those circumstances."

Lucas shifts uncomfortably in his seat, his gaze darting between Bishop and me. After a tense moment of silence, he takes a deep breath, and his shoulders slump as if a weight has been lifted off him.

"You're right," Lucas confesses, his voice barely above a whisper. "I did something I'm not proud of." He runs a hand through his hair nervously, avoiding our probing gazes. "But you have to understand how impossible it was for me to say no."

"Say no to what?"

He looks up. "They offered me fifty thousand dollars. Nobody would have turned that down."

"What was the money for?" Bishop asks.

Lucas shakes his head. "I figured you already knew.

They wanted me to steal information from the company I was working for."

"Manhattan AI?" I ask, remembering Lucas's picture in the article about the company.

Lucas nods and admits it, his voice filled with remorse. "It was one thumb drive . . . I didn't think it was a big deal."

"Corporate espionage," I state, allowing the words to settle over Lucas before speaking again. "Was Jason the one who hired you?"

"No. It was Declan," Lucas replies quickly. "Mr. McAllister never directly spoke to me about it."

As the pieces start falling into place, I can see the fear etched on Lucas's face. "Do you think there's any chance someone from Manhattan AI could have found out about what you did?" I inquire.

Lucas shakes his head adamantly. "No, no way. I was careful," he stammers out, his voice tinged

"You know that you committed a crime, don't you?" I inquire, hoping the weight of my question causes him to panic and perhaps reveal more to us than he intends.

The color drains from his face, and he stammers momentarily before blurting out, "I've never done anything else like that. It was just so much money."

Bishop raises an eyebrow. "But you knew it was wrong."

Lucas shifts uncomfortably before confessing, "My girlfriend's father warned me about even talking to anyone from Haven. I feel like such a fucking idiot that I didn't listen to him."

"Did he know Mr. McAllister?" I ask, curious about the revelation.

Lucas shakes his head. "Only by reputation. He's in real estate and knows a lot of people in the business world here. He told me Mr. McAllister didn't like to lose and had no problem making anyone he viewed as an enemy suffer."

"Is that why you killed him? Jason threatened to make you suffer?" I try to hide my surprise at Bishop's question.

"What?" Lucas exclaims, practically choking on his tongue. "You really think I had something to do with Mr. McAllister's death?"

I don't answer. I don't think Lucas was behind the murder, but I do believe he's keeping things from us. Perhaps Bishop's blunt approach to questioning is precisely what we need to pry the secrets out of Lucas that he doesn't seem to want to share.

Bishop shrugs. "Maybe someone from Manhattan AI got wind of what you did for Mr. McAllister. It's not a leap to think they told you to take care of the man or they would turn you in to the police."

The color drains from Lucas's face, leaving him ashen. "No, I swear. I didn't have anything to do with what happened to him. Oh fuck. Oh fuck. Oh fuck." Panic grips his voice. "Do you really think they found out? That they . . . that someone did something to Mr. McAllister because of me?"

"Could be," I say noncommittally, watching as the notion takes root in his mind. "It seems there was a lot of money in line with this deal that Haven was trying to close. Whatever you gave to your new boss must have been pretty valuable for them to give you such a large amount of cash."

Uncertainty flickers in his eyes like a deer caught in headlights. "I didn't think—I just . . ."

"You just took the money," I finish for him, standing up. "Think carefully. If there's anything else you haven't told me, now's the time."

Lucas nods, his mouth a tight line, his fingers knotted together. He's scared. It's written all over his face.

He swallows hard. "Look, I did it. I admit it. Declan approached me and told me the files they wanted from Manhattan AI. He told me they believed Manhattan AI had stolen some of their code base and needed the thumb drive to prove it. I thought what I was doing wasn't that bad because it was like stealing back what was already theirs. I didn't think it could put a target on Mr. McAllister's back."

"Declan told you that?" I ask.

Lucas nods. "I got it for them, then I started here but, I don't know, it just kind of freaked me out what they had me do, so when my girlfriend's dad told me if I got my real estate license, he would give me a job I decided it was the best move for me."

"And nobody at Haven knew you were planning to leave?"

"God, no. After everything I'd heard, I was scared to piss Mr. McAllister off. After I passed my test, I was going to give my notice. I went over to thank Victoria for her help that night." His eyes dart away, then back to mine. "But then everything—well, you know . . . I never got the chance."

"You're still here at Haven," I point out. "If you were going to quit, why didn't you?"

He shifts uncomfortably, his hands fidgeting with the hem of his shirt. "I-I was worried how it would look," he stammers. "After what happened, I don't know. I was afraid of what people might say."

"Like what?" I press.

He scoffs as if he can't believe I have to even ask the question. "Oh, I don't like it. Maybe if I leave, people will think I'm trying to hide that I was involved with whatever happened to Jason. I mean, hell, I'm already terrified my girlfriend is going to start believing all the rumors that I was sleeping with Victoria. The last thing I need is people saying I'm a murderer."

"Lucas," I say, my low voice unwavering, "you need to understand the seriousness of your situation. Corporate espionage is already a grave offense. If we find you are hiding anything else from us, I don't know if we can help you."

"Listen." He exhales sharply. "I've told you everything. I swear. Please, Detective Sanchez," he pleads. "I'm not a killer. I didn't have anything to do with what happened to Jason."

"I believe you," I admit, trying to put him at ease. Bishop eyes me with skepticism. "But you are at the center of this investigation, and I think you may know something without realizing you know it. You said Declan approached you about the job with Manhattan AI?"

Lucas nods. "Yes, everything that happened was between me and him. I didn't even realize Jason knew my name until he said good morning to me a couple of weeks ago."

"Do you think Jason was aware of what you took from Manhattan AI?" I wondered if we have been making assumptions about Jason being in control.

Lucas's brow furrows, and he blinks repeatedly, initially confused by my question. He shakes his head, "I-I don't know. I just assumed he was. But . . . never mind."

"No, tell us," I urge.

"Yeah, kid, it's a little late in this game for secrets," Bishop grumbles.

"Something strange happened with Declan once. I overheard him talking on the phone with someone, and he said something about wiping some sort of data. When he saw me approaching, he hurried and ended the call."

My heart quickens at this revelation. Could it be that Declan was involved in something sinister within Haven?

"Do you know who he was talking to?" I ask.

"No," Lucas admits. "And honestly, I didn't want to get involved."

Bishop crosses his arms, his expression cold and

calculating. "You sure managed to get involved in plenty of other trouble, didn't you?"

Lucas shakes his head; frustration is evident in his eyes. "I wish I could take it all back."

The room falls silent, the only sound the faint hum of the office outside the conference room. Lucas's shoulders slump as if a heavy burden weighs him down.

As the weight of the situation presses down on Lucas, I exchange a glance with Bishop. "If you truly want to make things right, Lucas, you have to start by telling the DA everything that happened."

"DA?" Lucas gulps.

"There is no avoiding the fact that you committed corporate espionage. If you tell the district attorney everything that happened, there's a chance you could get leniency," I explain.

"Oh my God, I am so fucked," Lucas mutters. "My girlfriend will never stay with me if I get arrested. What the hell am I going to do?"

Bishop and I stand to end the interview. I explain to Lucas again that his best option is to cooperate with the DA when he hears from them. In the meantime, he shouldn't hesitate to reach out if he thinks of anything else that might help us. As we head toward the exit, I stop suddenly when I hear Lucas's voice crack.

"D-Detectives," he starts, looking around the room sheepishly. "I don't know if it's important, but about a week ago, Declan called me into his office and told me I needed to stay away from Mrs. McAllister."

"He asked you to stay away from his partner's wife?" I ask.

Lucas nods. "I thought maybe Jason asked him to talk to me, but he seemed—I don't know . . . agitated that I was spending time with her. It's probably nothing, but you said you want me to tell you everything I know. That's all I'm trying to do."

Bishop and I exchange a glance filled with unspoken questions. Why would Declan be so insistent on Lucas keeping his distance from her? Was he protecting his partner, or could there have been more to their relationship than either let on?

I turn back to Lucas. "Thank you for sharing this with us."

Lucas nods fervently, his eyes wide with a mixture of fear and relief. Bishop and I step to the side, allowing Lucas to exit the conference room first. I grab Bishop's arm and wait for the glass door to fall shut again.

"What's up?" he asks, looking at me curiously.

"I think Declan is tied up in all of this a lot more than he's letting on," I state.

Bishop ponders my statement before asking, "So what are you thinking? He knew what Jason planned to do to his wife, so he warned Lucas to stay away from her."

"I don't know, but I say as long as we're here, we go ask him," I reply, a new determination setting in.

TWENTY-THREE

MARIA

Bishop follows close as we make our way toward Declan's office. When we approach, his gray-haired assistant looks up at us, her glasses shifting to the tip of her nose.

"Can I help you?" Her voice is sharp.

"We need a word with Mr. Harris," I state, my tone leaving no room for negotiation.

"Do you have an appointment?" she inquires, eyeing us up and down.

I flash her my badge and explain we have some questions to ask her boss.

"I don't care what you have to ask him; you can't just barge in here without making an appointment. Mr. Harris is a very busy man," the woman argues.

"It's alright," a voice calls from the office behind us. "I'm happy to talk to the detectives," Declan says smoothly, gesturing for us to enter.

The woman huffs, clearly agitated that she has been

overridden. As Bishop and I enter the office, a practiced smile stretches across his face, and the white teeth starkly contrast his tanned skin. "Detective Sanchez," he says, stepping forward and stretching a hand out. "And you are?"

"This is my partner," I begin before Bishop interjects.

"Detective Bishop."

"Nice to meet you." Declan asks, "Would you like anything to drink? Coffee, perhaps?"

"No, thank you," I reply, clipped and professional. Bishop adds he wouldn't mind a cup of coffee, and Declan quickly puts his assistant to work retrieving one for him.

"Mr. Harris," I say, my voice steady, "we need to talk about Jason."

"Jason?" He raises an eyebrow, feigning confusion as he leans back against the mahogany surface of his desk, arms folded. "Have you had a break in the case?"

"We know he was planning to murder his wife." My words are like bullets, direct and intended to hit their mark.

"Murder?" Declan blinks, a perfect picture of shock painting his face. "You think Jason . . . I can't believe it. He said things were better than ever between Victoria and him."

"I think you knew what he was planning to do." I lean forward, closing the distance between us.

"Detective, I assure you," he says, the surprise still plastered on his face, "this is the first I've heard of any homicidal intentions." His tone tries to thread the line between concern and innocence.

"Is that why you warned both Victoria and Lucas to stay away from each other?" I drop the question, watching for his reaction.

His Adam's apple bobs as he swallows, but he doesn't lose his composure. He's good at this game; I'll give him that.

"Jason may have told me that he was suspicious that Victoria was having an affair with Lucas, but that doesn't mean anything."

"Doesn't it?" I lean in again, pressing. "I don't see you getting tangled up in that mess unless you were worried about the fallout."

Declan's gaze locks with mine in a silent battle of wills. His lips part as if to counter, but then they seal shut, pressed into a thin line.

"Detective Sanchez," he finally says, drawing out each syllable, "I'm afraid you're looking for answers in the wrong place."

"Mr. Harris, you must take my partner and me as a couple of fools," Bishop adds.

"Excuse me?" Declan feigns insult just as his assistant enters and hands Bishop his coffee before exiting again.

"It's pretty clear that Jason confided in you about the affair," Bishop says before Declan interrupts him.

"I already told you that."

"Yes, but you didn't tell us that you had warned both Victoria and Lucas to stay away from each other.

Why would you do that unless you were worried about what Jason would do in response to finding out about their relationship?"

Declan's eyes flicker with something that resembles fear for a split second before his mask of composure slides back into place. "I was trying to defuse a volatile situation. That's it."

I cross my arms, unconvinced by his deflection. "So are you trying to say Jason never said anything to you that made you think maybe he was considering killing his wife?"

"If I had thought for a second that Jason would consider doing something like that, I would not have stood by and done nothing. Jason was aware that there is a divorce clause in our company bylines," Declan admits, his eyes darting between us.

"Divorce clause?" Bishop repeats.

"There's a clause in our company contract that if any executive level employees get divorced, a sale is initiated. The other majority shareholders would have the option to buy out any shares that would be at risk in the divorce," Declan explains. "But that doesn't mean Jason planned to hurt Victoria."

"You didn't think it was important to tell us Jason had a motive for murder?" I probe, watching his reaction closely.

"Of course not. Jason was the one who ended up dead, not Victoria," Declan replies defensively.

I raise an eyebrow at his defensive response, unconvinced by his attempt to divert suspicion. "Just because things didn't go as planned for Jason that night doesn't mean it's all not an important part of painting a complete picture."

"Yeah," Bishop jumps in. "And I bet Jason going off the deep end and murdering his wife probably wouldn't bode well for the sale of Haven you all are trying to push through, would it?"

Declan's jaw tightens at the mention of the sale. He shifts in his seat, fingers drumming nervously. "I may know more than I initially let on, but that doesn't make me complicit in any crime," he retorts, his tone defensive.

"Last I checked, corporate espionage is still a crime," I say.

Declan's façade breaks for a split second, a flash of panic crossing his features before he schools his expression back into neutrality. "I don't know what you're talking about," he says with forced calmness.

"You had to know Lucas would tell us everything. He claims you were the one who approached him. In fact, he went as far as to say you were the only one he ever dealt with and that Jason had no involvement as far as he knew," I push back.

"Lucas is a liar," Declan responds a little too quickly. "He's trying to shift blame because he knows he's probably going away for murder."

"You know what I think? I think you were aware of what was happening. Jason's growing paranoia, the divorce clause, and the impending sale—it was all too much pressure. Maybe you didn't want to get your hands dirty directly, but turning a blind eye is just as bad."

Declan's façade cracks, his eyes darting around the room for a moment before landing back on me with a mix of defiance and fear. "Well, detectives, you will have to excuse me. I have a busy day. I suggest you contact our lawyers if you need anything else." He dismisses us, his tone icy.

My partner, Bishop, shifts beside me. We both know Declan's retreat behind his lawyer's skirts is as close to an admission as we're likely to get today.

"Very well," I concede, standing. "We'll be in touch."

Bishop nods at me, and we walk out of the office.

Declan's assistant avoids eye contact as we stride through the outer office, her fingers clacking on the keyboard in a rapid staccato.

"Sanchez," Bishop murmurs, "that guy is definitely hiding something."

I agree with him as we exit into the corridor. We've rattled Declan, but not enough to shatter his composure completely. Not yet.

As we stand and wait for the elevator, I glance down at my phone. The screen lights up with an alert that snags my attention—a missed call from Victoria.

"Mrs. McAllister called," I murmur, thumbing the voicemail icon. The message plays low, just a whisper of sound, but her urgency slices through the quiet. "Detective Sanchez, this is Victoria McAllister. I'm sorry to bother you so soon, but there's something else I think we need to talk about. Please call me as soon as you're available."

"Wonder what that's about," Bishop says, his eyes sharp on me, reading the concern etching its way across my face.

"I don't know." I slip the phone back into my pocket. "But she sounded worried."

"You should probably follow up with her," Bishop says, nodding. "Drop me at the precinct first, and I'll head over to Manhattan AI and see exactly who knew what."

"Good call," I admit.

The elevator doors slide open with a soft chime. As we descend, a heavy silence settles between us. Bishop leans against the wall, his gaze fixed on the shifting numbers above the door.

"You think Victoria knows more than she's letting on?" he asks, breaking the silence.

I consider his question carefully, mulling over the cryptic urgency in her voice. "It's possible. My gut says she's not telling us something."

Bishop nods in agreement. "Maybe she's finally ready to start telling the truth."

Victoria's message is in my mind, and I can't argue that Bishop is wrong about her.

TWENTY-FOUR

MARIA

When we arrive at the precinct, Bishop takes the car, and I head inside, prepared to return Victoria McAllister's call. I barely make it inside the door before my phone vibrates. I hastily look at the message, expecting it to be Victoria, but it's the chief instead.

The text message reads: Sanchez, my office, now.

I grimace as I reluctantly make my way toward the chief's office. As I enter, the chief gestures for me to take a seat and gets straight to the point.

"What's going on with the McAllister case?" he asks, eyeing me.

"We're working on it," I answer matter-of-factly.

"Yeah, I assumed that much. I need something to tell the mayor," he states, his tone clipped.

A surge of frustration bubbles within me as I resist the urge to snap back a retort. "I can't work the case any faster than the evidence allows. Besides, I don't work for the mayor." As soon as the words leave my mouth, I want to kick myself for being unable to resist the snipe.

The chief's steely gaze meets mine, unwavering. "No, you answer to me. And I, in turn, answer to him."

Reluctantly I nod, acknowledging the chain of command. The chief leans back in his chair, folding his hands together.

"Now, where are we with this case?" he asks briskly.

I launch into a detailed rundown of the suspects and evidence gathered so far, knowing he won't be pleased with our progress before I finish.

The chief listens intently, his expression unreadable.

"Is there any chance this could have been a random act of violence? Or maybe McAllister had an accident, tripped, and fell on his own gun?" he questions.

I let out a disbelieving laugh. "Are you serious?"

"What about suicide?" he pushes further, crossing his arms. "We can't rule it out, especially with the pressure he was under."

"He was hit in the back of the head with something and then shot in the chest. I'm pretty sure we can rule out suicide." I can't hide the fact that I think the conversation we're having is absurd. "Sir, we are working as fast as we can. We'll get to the bottom of this."

"In the meantime, I'm dealing with the mayor, who tells me his phone is ringing off the hook from wealthy donors who are worried they could be next," Chief explains. "You have to remember that these people are thinking if someone like Jason McAllister isn't safe in his own home, then who is?"

"That's ridiculous. This was obviously not a random act of violence," I argue.

"And you don't believe it was his wife or this Lucas Flynn individual?" he asks, eyes fixed on my face.

"Think about it," I press on, turning to face them both. "The timing, the method—it was surgical, calculated. Whoever did this knew what Jason was planning and used it against him." My voice is firm and resolute.

I'm barely catching my breath when Chief leans forward, his fingers laced together on the desk that has seen more than its fair share of buried cases and solved mysteries. "I know you and Bishop are working the case, but we need to wrap this up, Sanchez," he says, his voice echoing a weariness from too many years of public service. "The community is rattled. They want answers, and they want them yesterday."

I nod, even though every fiber in me screams that rushing this could mean missing something crucial. I hate the fact that the wealthy of this city have a direct line to the mayor. The level of inequality among the haves and have-nots in this city is staggering. "Understood, Chief. The more I dig into Declan Harris, the more I think he could be the key to this case."

"About that," the chief continues. "The mayor didn't reach out because he wanted an update. Apparently, Mr. Harris called him to complain that some detectives were at his place of business, harassing him."

"We what?" I spit out the words, shock and disbelief consuming me. "That fucking piece of shit," I growl.

"What did you think would happen, Sanchez?" the

chief's voice is sharp, his eyes narrowing on me. "You know these guys have connections in high places. You can't just roll in there tossing around accusations without evidence."

"I didn't expect him to run to the mayor like a child tattling on us," I seethe, the frustration boiling beneath the surface. "I know he knew that McAllister was planning to kill his wife."

"Well, she's alive, and he's not," Chief states. "Don't go at Harris again without something more concrete, understand?"

I swallow my retort, clenching my jaw tightly as I nod, the taste of defeat bitter in my mouth. "Understood, Chief," I reply evenly, trying to keep my frustration from leaking into my voice.

As I rise from the chair, ready to leave the chief's office, I remember Victoria McAllister's message waiting for me. Perhaps I will get lucky, and she will have the break I have been waiting for.

With a curt nod, I exit the office and head back to my desk. Reaching for my notepad, I dial Victoria's number, trying to push the frustration from my conversation with Chief deep down inside myself.

Victoria picks up after several rings; her voice is soft and trembling. "Detective Sanchez, thank you for getting back to me."

"Of course," I reply. "Did you remember something?"

"Actually . . ." She hesitates, and I sense a bit of fear in her voice. "Is there any way we can meet?"

"Of course. At your hotel?"

"No!" she exclaims a little too eagerly. "Actually, I'm not far from the precinct."

"You're not?"

"No, but I would prefer not to be seen walking in there. I'm sitting at a little café around the corner, The Blue Latte."

"I know it," I reply.

"Could you come now?" she asks, her tone almost desperate.

Without hesitation, I reply, "I'll be there in fifteen minutes." I hang up the phone and grab my coat eagerly.

Arriving at The Blue Latte, I spot Victoria sitting by the window, her hands wrapped tightly around a steaming cup of coffee. She looks up as I approach, her eyes red-rimmed with tears threatening to spill over.

"Thank you for coming, Detective," she says quietly before gesturing for me to take a seat across from her.

I sit down, my gaze locked on hers. "Victoria, what's wrong?"

She looks away from me before whispering, "Jason's death. It's all my fault."

The café is filled with the murmur of voices and the clinking of dishes, but at that moment, it feels like it's just the two of us. Victoria's admission hangs heavy in the air, and for a moment, I'm taken aback by her words.

"Your fault?" I ask gently, trying to keep my tone soothing. "What did you do?"

She nods, tears still streaming down her face. "I knew he was planning something, but I never thought . . . I never imagined . . ."

As I look at Victoria, my stomach tightens as her words sink in. Leaning forward, I reach out and touch her trembling hand gently.

"Victoria, you need to tell me everything," I urge, my voice soft yet insistent.

She sniffles, composing herself before she speaks. "I'll tell you everything."

TWENTY-FIVE

MARIA

"What do you mean it was your fault?" I ask, refusing to shift my eyes away from Victoria.

She blinks rapidly, her eyes darting away before settling on my face again. There's a palpable tension between us.

"Jason . . . I knew what kind of man he was," she whispers, the words trembling on the edge of a sob. "But I did it anyway."

I study her closely, noting the quiver in her lip and how her hands twist together in her lap. Fear? Guilt? It's hard to pinpoint, but whatever it is, it gnaws at her from the inside out.

"What did you do?" I ask, my voice steady. Is this a confession? Was I wrong? Did Victoria kill her husband?

Her shoulders were hunched as if bracing against an invisible blow. At that moment, she's obviously wrestling with something dark and tangled. Something that, once it grips your soul, doesn't easily let go.

I keep quiet, giving her space to piece together her thoughts. The silence stretches, heavy and expectant. Finally, she looks up again, her eyes haunted.

"It's my fault because I knew what he was capable of," she admits, a tremble in her voice betraying the fear that claws at her resolve. "I should have left when I found out about all the women. But I stayed and did the exact thing I knew would drive him mad."

"Go on," I encourage gently, aware of the delicate balance between pushing too hard and not enough.

"And now he's dead," she finishes in barely a whisper. "It feels like my fault because I should have seen it coming."

I nod, understanding the complexity of guilt and how it can wrap around the heart and squeeze.

"Let's take it step by step," I suggest, offering a semblance of control. "Are you talking about Lucas? Were you not telling us the truth when you said there wasn't an affair?"

She shakes her head, lifting a tissue to blow her nose. She takes a deep breath, steadying herself.

Victoria's gaze flits about the room, touching everything except me. I need to bring her back and ground her in the here and now.

"Victoria," I say, my voice soft but firm, "it's okay. You can tell me the truth."

She blinks, surprised by the directness, then shakes

her head vehemently. "I did tell you the truth. Lucas is just a friend, nothing more."

"Okay, I believe you." Trust is currency in this room; I give it willingly if it means getting to the truth. I watch her relax marginally at my words, her shoulders dropping from around her ears. "It's crucial we establish a clear picture of your relationships. This helps us eliminate possible motives and suspects."

She nods, a hesitation flickering in her eyes—a sign that there's more to unearth.

"Is there something else? Someone else?" I prod gently yet unrelentingly. The puzzle pieces are here; I just need her to turn them over.

She releases a breath like she's surrendering her last secret. "Yes."

"Who is he?" My question slices into the pause, clean and precise.

"It's been over for a while," she says, avoiding my question.

"Okay. Who was it?"

She swallows hard and avoids looking at me as she whispers her confession, "Declan Harris." Her fingers knot together as if she's trying to hold herself steady. "But it ended six months ago. It has nothing to do with Jason's death. At least—I didn't think it did."

There's a vulnerability in her posture as I reply, "We can't rule anything out."

Her eyes meet mine, flickers of fear dancing within. "I understand," she whispers. But does she really grasp the gravity of her revelation?

The distant look in her eyes tells me she's not really here with me but lost in some memory.

"Tell me about your relationship with Declan," I prompt.

"I know it's no excuse, but it's hard to be in Jason's sphere sometimes. He has such high expectations of everyone he surrounds himself with," she begins.

"I can see how hard that must be."

"I went to Declan about eighteen months ago when I started to have suspicions that Jason was cheating on me again. I needed someone to confirm I wasn't crazy, ya know?"

I did know. I was her once. I was the wife who was repeatedly told I was insecure and paranoid. "And Declan was that person for you?"

She nods. "He was a good friend to me during a really tough time. He made me feel seen and heard when I felt like I was going crazy."

I nod, understanding the allure of being validated. "And he confirmed Jason was cheating?"

"Not right away, but eventually."

"When did your relationship with him change?"

Her eyes cloud with remorse. "It just . . . happened. Slowly and then all at once. He listened to me and showed me kindness, which I felt was lacking in my marriage."

"And Jason?" I prod gently.

Victoria looks away, her voice barely above a whisper as she confesses, "Jason didn't know. He couldn't know. It would have been . . . catastrophic."

"Do you think there's a chance he ever found out about you and Declan?"

"No." She shakes her head vigorously. "No way. We would have known."

"Did Declan have any reason to want Jason out of the picture?"

Her eyes widened in alarm, and disbelief was written all over her face. "No! Declan is not capable of . . . that!"

"People can surprise you," I say evenly, watching her reaction.

She slumps back into the couch, her gaze distant as if lost in contemplation or guilt. "Maybe . . . but he warned me about Lucas because he wanted to protect me."

"Or," I counter gently, "maybe he had his own motives. Perhaps Declan couldn't stand the idea of you being with someone else. How did Declan react when the relationship ended?"

Victoria shakes her head slowly. "He took it hard. Declan didn't want it to end. He said he needed me." She wraps her arms around herself as if the memory chills her.

"And after?" I lean forward slightly. "How did he behave once it was over?"

Her unease is palpable. "At first, he kept calling and showing up at places he knew I'd be. I thought he just needed closure. But eventually, I told him if he didn't stop, I would have to tell Jason."

"And did that work?"

She nods. "I thought it did." She trails off, and I can see the effort it takes for her to continue.

"What's changed?" I press. "What made you call me?"

She sighs. "I called you today because when I said I wasn't having an affair, I couldn't shake the guilt of the lie. I'm really not sleeping with Lucas, but that doesn't change what I did. Now, all I can think of is what would have happened if Jason had found out. What if that was why he came there that night to kill me?"

"I don't think Jason was there to kill you because of your relationship with Declan. From everything I know, he was convinced you were having a relationship with Lucas," I explain, hoping my words give her peace of mind.

"Well, after I left the message for you, Declan contacted me."

"Did you tell him you were going to tell me about the affair?"

"No!" Victoria exclaims. "He called me because he said he knew I was talking to people and that if I knew what was good for me, I would keep my mouth shut. His tone was different, colder."

"Did he threaten you?" The question is out before I can weigh its impact.

"No, not outright." Victoria's voice shakes,

betraying the fear she's trying to contain. "I barely recognized him. It scared me."

My hand instinctively rests on the notepad in my lap, a silent reminder of my role here. I lean forward. "We can provide protection for you, but it's crucial that you make an official statement."

Her eyes flit to the door as if contemplating escape but then resolutely return to mine. Her hands are clasped tightly, knuckles whitening with each passing second.

"Protection?" she echoes, the word hollow, like she's trying it on for size. "You really think Declan is dangerous?"

"I think as women, men in our lives tell us not to trust our guts, but sometimes our instincts are right. Declan's behavior is concerning, and we can't underestimate the lengths someone will go to when feeling threatened," I explain in a calming yet serious tone.

She inhales sharply, a silent gasp, and I see the weight of my words. Her gaze drifts away, focusing on some unseen point in the distance as she contemplates the implications.

"Could . . . could Declan really be involved?" she asks, her voice barely above a whisper, as if saying it louder might make it true.

"I don't know," I confess because honesty is the only foundation we can build on right now.

"But he was in San Francisco that night."

"You thought Jason was too," I remind her.

"Oh my God." She exhales. "I can't believe this is happening."

"Listen to me," I say, locking eyes with her. "We are going to do everything in our power to protect you. You have my word on that."

Her gaze flutters toward me, and for a moment, I see the flicker of hope amid the storm of her emotions. She nods. I can tell she wants to believe me; she needs to believe me. It's etched in the lines of her face, the way she holds herself—poised on the brink of either breaking down or finding the courage to stand strong.

"I need you to come back to the precinct and make an official statement on the record about your relationship with Declan and everything he has said to you. We can go through the rear entrance of the station. Nobody needs to know you were there," I assure her.

"Thank you, Detective Sanchez," she says, her voice stronger now. "For believing me. For everything."

TWENTY-SIX

MARIA

My buzzing phone cuts through the silence like a warning siren, and I snatch it up, half expecting another dead end or, worse, a new crisis. It's Bishop. His voice comes through, tinged with an urgency that sets my nerves on edge.

"Sanchez, you sitting down? Just left a chat with Sam Littleton over at Manhattan AI."

I'm not sitting down but leaning against my desk, bracing myself. "Talk to me."

"Turns out, the intel Lucas gave Declan—it was a plant," he says, words paced for impact. "Sam gave me the lowdown on it all. Apparently, Jason found out that Declan had lost confidence in him finishing the AI model before the deadline. He had Declan followed and figured out what he was up to."

"He what?"

"I know, right?" Bishop gasps. "Sam says that Jason reached out to him directly and said he wanted to teach

Declan a lesson. He gave Sam the name of one of his employees that Declan had been seen meeting with, and that's how he knew what to feed Lucas."

A chill snakes down my spine. A plant. My mind races, trying to connect the dots that keep multiplying and shifting, elusive as shadows. "But why? What's the point of screwing over your business partner like that or risking that Sam will report Declan to the police?"

"I think McAllister cared more about the loyalty of the people around him than thinking ahead about the consequences of the things he did," Bishop replies.

"Christ." My hand goes to my temple, fingers massaging as if I could knead the confusion into something coherent. "Lucas unknowingly feeds Declan fake data, and Jason ends up dead. None of this makes sense."

"Maybe we're looking at this all wrong. Maybe it's not about the data itself but what the data represents—"

"What do you mean?"

"Declan doing what he did meant he had no faith in Jason. Maybe that was more than Jason could tolerate," Bishop replies.

"That would make sense if Declan was the one who ended up dead. Dammit! None of this adds up." I push away from the desk, restless energy coursing through me. "We've got motives for days, but none of it matches the crime scene."

"It's clear that Jason didn't trust his business partners, so I'm not sure how much he would have shared with him about his plans to off his wife," Bishop says.

"Well, things are even more complicated than you think. While you were checking into Manhattan AI, I met with Victoria McAllister. She told me while she didn't have an affair with Lucas, she was involved in a relationship with Declan for nearly a year."

"Are you fucking kidding me?"

"Apparently, she ended it six months ago, but she said Declan called her and warned her not to tell anyone about their relationship," I continued.

Bishop's sharp intake of breath crackles through the line. "So Declan was involved with Victoria?"

"Seems that way," I confirm.

"Jesus. This just keeps getting crazier."

"To make matters worse, the chief says we can't touch Declan without concrete evidence. We're drowning in motives, but nothing solid to tie it all together."

"We need to start connecting these dots, Sanchez," Bishop states what I already am fully aware of.

I nod resolutely even though he can't see me through the phone. "Agreed. Based on what Victoria told me, I didn't think it was just a fling for Declan. Something tells me he may have actually had feelings for her."

"Sound like you think he did this?" Bishop asks. "But let's not forget that Declan has an alibi. He was all the way up in San Francisco when Jason took his last breath."

"Or so he says," I echo, but it's hollow and unconvincing even to my own ears. "But Jason proved that an alibi can be faked. We need to see if we can figure out if anyone saw him in the evening after Jason left."

"There's also the chance he hired someone to do it —" Bishop murmurs.

"If it was Declan, I still can't figure out how he thought it would all go down. No way did Jason tell him the details of his plans. He wouldn't have known that Jason knocked Victoria out, which means he would be risking Victoria seeing him at the house," I state, thinking out loud rather than looking for an answer.

"Jealousy is a powerful thing," Bishop notes, his tone contemplative. "It can drive a man to do unthinkable things. Maybe he couldn't take Jason having everything he wanted anymore."

"It's all circumstantial. Victoria's confession, the planted data—it's suggestive, not definitive," I reply. "No way does the chief give us the go-ahead on Declan with a mountain of circumstantial."

"Fine. Then we start with poking holes in his alibi. San Francisco PD owes me a favor or two," Bishop muses, a smirk tugging at the edge of his lips. "I'll call and see if they can help me with some hotel staff interviews."

"Meanwhile, I'll revisit the forensic reports, dive deeper into the financials, anything we can use to layer against Declan," I add.

The phone call ends with a silent promise between Bishop and me to crack this case wide open. I gather my notes and head straight for the parking lot. It's time for me to head home and be a mom again. As I walk through the precinct, I continue to try to make sense of all the pieces of evidence. As much as everything points toward Declan, I can't shake the idea that we're missing something.

From everything I have seen in this case, there is no question that Jason McAllister was a ruthless narcissist. As I drive home, the pieces of the puzzle refuse to align neatly in my mind. Jason's shadow looms large over this investigation. The darkness of his secrets seems to seep into every corner of these people's lives.

When I walk through the threshold of my home, my daughter's laughter tinkles down the hallway, reminding me why I work so hard.

"Hey, criminal," I tease. "How was your last day of suspension?"

"I hopped on an empty train car, robbed a convenience store, and tore all the tags off our mattresses, so it feels like it was a pretty productive day." Jordan's sense of humor is the only thing I'm glad she got from her father.

I chuckle, grateful for her levity in the midst of the darkness that seems to swallow me whole some days. "Well, just don't leave any fingerprints, okay?" I quip back.

Jordan grins and rolls her eyes, the tension that had momentarily gripped my chest loosening with her familiar sass. She tosses her backpack onto the couch and plops down beside it. "Anything interesting happen today with the case?" she asks, her curiosity mirrored in the glint of her eyes.

"You know I can't talk about it."

Jordan leans forward, eager for details. "Oh, come on, who am I going to tell?"

I give her a playful side-eye, knowing full well that my daughter can extract information from me when she puts her mind to it. "Nice try, Jordan," I counter, with a smirk tugging at the corner of my lips.

"Fine," she huffs dramatically, flopping back against the couch in mock defeat. "But you know I'm great at reading people. I can practically see the gears turning in your head right now."

I chuckle, impressed by her perceptiveness but unwilling to divulge any details that could compromise the investigation. "You've got your father's charm, that's for sure. Maybe someday you'll put it to good use as a detective," I tease gently.

"No thanks," she says as she raises an eyebrow. "Well, if you need an extra set of eyes, you know where to find me."

"Thanks, kiddo," I reply softly, reaching out to ruffle her hair affectionately.

The image of Declan Harris looms large in my thoughts. His connection to Victoria, his possible obsession with her. As much as my mind wants to work out the puzzle in my head, I force his face from my thoughts and turn to my daughter.

"How about we go out for pizza tonight?" I offer.

Jordan's eyes light up at the mention of pizza; her earlier curiosity shifted to excitement. "Yes, please! I'm craving that new place with the garlic knots," she exclaims.

I follow her, a smile playing on my lips as I watch her bound with youthful energy. Amid life's chaos, these simple moments with my daughter offer a reprieve, a glimpse of normalcy.

TWENTY-SEVEN

MARIA

Unplugging for an evening at home with my daughter has done exactly as I had hoped. I awoke today with a fresh perspective on the case. Certain things about the case are clear. Jason McAllister had every intention of murdering his wife on the night he met his end. That much is evident by the fact he meticulously curated an alibi and even went so far as to spike the champagne he knew his wife would drink.

The more I dig into Mr. McAllister's life, the more the suspect list grows. Lucas, Victoria, and Declan all had motives for wanting the man dead. Bishop seems ready to accept Declan Harris, who either managed to slip away to commit the crime or hired someone to carry it out. While he is a viable suspect, something tells me we have yet to uncover a number of additional suspects. I was up before sunrise today with one clear thought about where to start. The man Jason McAllister hires to make all his problems go away.

My thumb hits the call button. It feels like hours before the line finally clicks and Marshall Scott's voice comes through.

"Mr. Scott? This is Detective Sanchez."

"Sanchez?" he answers, his tone barely audible over what sounds like industrial fans whirling in the background.

"Yes, the detective working on the Jason McAllister murder."

"Ah, yes, good morning, Detective," he says. "How can I help you?"

"Are you back in town? I would love to have this discussion in person," I inquire, still struggling to hear the man through the noise on his end of the line.

He is silent for a few moments before he rattles off a place and time he can meet me later this morning. I end the call and continue driving toward the station, mulling over the dozens of questions I have for the "fixer."

TWENTY-EIGHT

MARIA

As I drive through the city streets, lost in my thoughts surrounding the case, I flinch at the sound of my phone. An unknown number flashes on the dashboard display.

I press the button on the hands-free display and answer. "Detective Sanchez speaking."

"Detective, it's Jenny—Jenny Mayweather, Jason's assistant." Her voice quivers like a plucked violin string, high-pitched and trembling.

"Jenny," I acknowledge, keeping my tone level though my pulse ticks up a notch. "What can I do for you?"

A pause stretches just long enough to become uncomfortable. I hear her breathe, a shaky inhale followed by a stuttered exhale. "I'm sorry to bother you . . . It's just . . . I don't know what to do."

My grip on the steering wheel loosens just a fraction, the leather creaking under my hands. "Jenny," I start, my voice steady but insistent, "whatever it is, you can tell me. Is it about Jason?"

A beat of silence passes before she replies. "Yes, and . . . and Mr. Harris." Her words are halting, like she's picking her way across a minefield. "It's something that happened before—before Jason left for LA."

"Go on," I urge, my curiosity piqued.

"I can't help but feel like I shouldn't be telling anyone this. He's still my boss." Jenny's thoughts begin to wander.

"Jenny, you clearly felt compelled to call me about whatever is bothering you. Trust your gut, okay?"

I hear a heavy sigh through the line before she continues. "Mr. Harris called me the night that—well, the night that Jason—" Her voice cracks, and she pauses before continuing. "Well, you know. Mr. Harris asked me to send him Jason's pitch deck for the following morning. He wanted it emailed directly to him."

"Okay . . ." I prompt, waiting for her to connect the dots. "And was this out of the ordinary?"

"Jason was supposed to be there with him. Why ask me to send it? I told him Jason had a copy, and he said he didn't want to bother him." Her voice is a low whisper now.

"I see."

There's a pause on the line—a soft intake of breath as if she's bracing herself. "Detective Sanchez," Jenny starts, and I can hear the tremble in her voice, "I think . . . I think Declan might have known that Jason would be driving back to LA, and he wanted me to send that report because he knew he wouldn't be coming back."

The car swerves slightly as my concentration falters, and I right it with a jerk.

"Jenny," I say, my voice steady despite the turmoil inside, "that's a serious accusation. Is there something that makes you say that?"

Jenny takes a moment before replying, "I didn't think much of it at the time, but now . . . with everything that happened, I don't know."

"Thank you for telling me this," I say.

"Detective Sanchez, am I being paranoid? What if it's just a coincidence?" Jenny's voice wavers.

I take a deep breath, trying to reassure her despite my own suspicions. "Jenny, you did the right thing by bringing this to my attention."

"Thank you, Detective Sanchez," she musters a whisper of gratitude, but the tremble hasn't left her voice. "I just want this nightmare to end."

"And I'm going to do everything in my power to see that it does," I promise before ending the call.

Every time I try to convince myself it's too convenient for Declan to be the one behind Jason's murder, something else happens, adding another layer to the man's motive. Perhaps I'm the one who is overthinking things, and the most obvious conclusion is, in fact, the correct one.

I start heading toward the location where I'm supposed to meet Marshall Scott. The clarity I had woken up with is starting to fade as my mind races with Jenny's revelation.

Pulling into a parking spot along the street, I grab my phone and craft a text to my partner, Bishop. I told him I was about to have an interview with the fixer, Mr. Scott, and would head back to the precinct afterward to debrief him on everything I discovered.

I roll my eyes when Bishop doesn't type a reply and instead just gives my text a thumbs-up. Part of me thought perhaps he would offer to meet me for the meeting with Marshall, but I know better. Bishop is about as good at having a partner as I am.

As I step out of my car and approach the designated meeting spot with Marshall, a thought pops into my mind. This man didn't just work for Mr. McAllister. He worked for anyone who paid him. It's not far-fetched to think there is even the chance that Mr. Scott himself could have been the one who pulled the trigger that night at the behest of someone else.

He says he works within the confines of the law, but I think anyone who has spoken to Mr. Scott knows that is probably far from the truth. This case has my head spinning. I have never had a victim that made me think anyone who had contact with him would probably want him dead.

I exhale a large breath as I try to remind myself that while Jason McAllister was a deplorable human being, everyone deserves justice at the end of the day.

TWENTY-NINE

MARIA

I arrive before Marshall at the small bodega. I've never been to the establishment, but it gives off the vibes of a business that has been a neighborhood presence for decades. I make my way to a small table in the rear and take a seat facing the door so I can see Mr. Marshall when he enters.

He's late. In fact, he was so late that I tried calling him, but he didn't pick up. Finally, when he arrives, his appearance is disheveled and not what I had imagined when I spoke to the man on the phone.

"Detective Sanchez, I presume," he says as he approaches, and I stand, shaking his hand. He waves to the man behind the counter, who, without a word, brings us two cups of coffee. Immediately, I understand this is a place where Marshall feels at home. These people know him, and I wonder what he has "fixed" for them.

"I was starting to think you weren't going to show," I state as I take my seat.

He chuffs before sitting and heaping a sugar mountain into his coffee. "You and me both. Sorry for my appearance; I had a stakeout that lasted overnight. I intended to shower before our meeting, but my morning had other plans."

I can't help but wonder how many secrets this man keeps inside his head. He's who the rich and powerful in the city call to make their problems disappear. As much as he likes to say he does it within the confines of the law, we both know he wouldn't be in such demand if that were true.

"Mr. Scott—"

"Call me Marshall. Everyone does."

I nod. "Marshall. I need to ask you about a few of Jason McAllister's . . . dealings," I say, my gaze unwavering.

"I assumed."

"My partner spoke to Sam Littleton, who informed us that Jason McAllister gave him a heads-up about Declan Harris's plans to commit corporate espionage."

Marshall chuckles in response to my words. "That guy is such a fuckup."

"Mr. Littleton?"

Marshall shakes his head. "No, Declan. That guy is his own worst enemy, and McAllister was fully aware of what a fuckup his partner was."

"Really? Do you think there's a chance that Declan found out that Jason slipped him fake data?" I inquire.

Marshall furrows his brow in confusion. "Declan knew. Jason told him." He laughs again. "Fuck, no way in a million years would McAllister not taunt that man with what he did. But that was how the man worked. He loved teaching people lessons, as he called it."

"Wait, what?"

Marshall sighed before launching into an explanation. "While following Declan, I saw him meet with that Lucas kid. I reported everything back to Jason, who then came up with the idea of looping Sam into his plan."

"How did this teach Declan a lesson?"

"Who do you think paid Lucas?" Marshall continues. "Declan didn't want Jason to find out that he didn't have faith that he would finish the code base in time, so he paid Lucas from his personal funds. After it was done, Jason told Declan he knew everything. He also told him that since he hired the kid, Lucas's payroll would also come directly out of Declan's pocket."

"How did Declan take all of this?"

Marshall takes a sip of his coffee before continuing. "Well, he wasn't too pleased, to say the least. But Jason had this way about him, Detective. He always knew exactly what strings to pull to keep control of the situation."

"You said you followed Declan for a bit?" I ask, and Marshall nods in response. "In that time, did you ever become aware that Mrs. McAllister and Mr. Harris were having an affair?"

Marshall slumps back in his seat. "No shit?"

"Mrs. McAllister confirmed it herself but said it ended at least six months ago."

Marshall shakes his head. "It must have already ended when Jason asked me to tail him, but that all makes sense now."

"What does?"

"A few times when I followed Declan, he would park outside Mrs. McAllister's gym or at a restaurant where she was having lunch. I thought it was weird that he was following her, but these fucking people, who knows why they do what they do."

"Did you tell Jason his partner was following his wife?" I ask.

He shakes his head. "Not exactly; I just gave him a report listing where he was and when. I can't say if he pieced anything together or not."

I take a moment to process Marshall's revelations, feeling like I'm finally starting to get a picture of who Jason McAllister was. "Marshall, thank you for sharing all this with me. I know your specialty is keeping secrets buried, and I want you to know that anything you share with me will be kept confidential."

"Just ask your question, Detective. Don't try handling me, okay?"

I nod, acknowledging Marshall's request. "Did Jason McAllister ever mention his plans regarding Declan Harris?" I ask, locking eyes with the fixer.

Marshall leans back in his chair, contemplating his response for a moment. "Jason wasn't one to spill all of his schemes, but I can tell you after everything that happened, he didn't trust Declan," he admits.

"It seems like Jason McAllister didn't trust many people."

Marshall chuckles. "You could say that, but at the end of the day, Jason was a complicated man."

"What do you mean?"

"I think the main reason he didn't trust people was because he thought everyone thought like him. He was always calculating and maneuvering, but most people aren't that complicated," Marshall explains.

"I have to admit, every time I find a new connection to Mr. McAllister, the suspect list seems to get longer and longer. In your dealings with him, is there anyone else you can think of that we should be looking into?" I ask, and I'm almost certain of the non-answer I'm about to receive.

Marshall takes a long sip of his coffee before responding, his eyes darting away momentarily. "Jason played his cards close to the chest, Detective. Sorry I can't help you more."

I wish I could crack this guy's skull open like a coconut and reveal the thousands of secrets I know are swimming around in there.

"I understand. Thank you for all your help today." I stand, shake his hand, and make my exit, knowing I've gotten as much from the man as I am going to.

THIRTY

MARIA

The moment I push through the precinct doors, a current of tension hits me like the first wave of an oncoming storm. My gaze instinctively sweeps across the room, landing on the chief's closed door. Through the frosted glass, two shadows move—one tall and imposing, the other stocky and assertive. Bishop is in there with the chief.

Without missing a beat, I stride toward my desk, trying to appear unbothered. I've barely settled in when the door swings open. Bishop emerges, his eyes locking onto me with the precision of a targeting system. He gives a curt nod, signaling me to join them.

"Sanchez," the chief's voice booms as I enter, an unspoken command reverberating in the single word. His face is granite-hard, and his eyes are fixed on mine.

"Take a seat," he says, not as an invitation but as an order. I comply. Bishop stands to the side, arms folded, his expression unreadable.

"Chief?" I start. "If this is about the McAllister case, I've—"

"Bishop here was telling me that Declan Harris has become the focus of the investigation," the chief starts without preamble. "It sounds like a mountain of evidence exists against the man."

"I don't think I would exactly put it that way, sir," I reply, my words laced with skepticism. "He certainly is the most viable option at this point, but it doesn't seem like we have enough for a conviction. Everything up until this point is pretty circumstantial," I explain.

"Actually, Sanchez, while you were out this morning, there have been a few developments," Bishop interjects. I look up at him, surprise registering on my face.

"I wasn't out," I huff before clarifying. "I was interviewing people connected to the case."

"Well, wherever you were," Bishop continues with the wave of a hand. "I had a very enlightening chat with the concierge at the hotel, who informed me that he saw Mr. Harris exit the hotel at nine fifteen p.m. and did not notice him returning."

"Not noticing him returning doesn't mean he didn't," I point out, unable to explain why I can't seem to wrap my head around Declan being the culprit behind Jason's demise.

"I'm not done," Bishop continues. "The techs were also able to finally get into Mr. McAllister's phone."

"They what?" I gasp, my head snapping toward Bishop, my face flushing hot with anger. "Why didn't you call me?"

"I was here working the evidence, Sanchez. I can't constantly worry about trying to keep you in the loop," Bishop grunts. My fists ball at my sides, my knuckles turning white.

"What did they find on his phone?" I ask, pushing past my anger.

"Let me see," the chief says, looking at a piece of paper in front of him. "You're done, Jason. I'll make sure you regret crossing me."

"Then there is the one sent two days before Jason's death that said you won't get away with this," Bishop adds.

"Threats don't always translate to action," I point out. "Jason pissed a lot of people off, and there were a lot who wanted him dead. It just feels like if it were Declan, there would be some sort of smoking gun."

The pieces click together, an image forming that's hard to dismiss. Yet in the back of my mind, uncertainties still swirl. Evidence should be irrefutable, but this feels like assembling a puzzle with corners forced to fit.

"I understand your concern, Sanchez, but the mayor wants this wrapped up sooner rather than later. He's not going to like us pointing the finger at another member of the company, but I think he would still prefer we put this case to bed," the chief says. "I'm going to run this by the prosecutor. With these messages, the testimony about Declan's early night, and all the other things we have tied him to, I want to know if he thinks we've got enough to consider pressing charges."

But something within me resists, a tug at the hem of my conscience. "Chief," I say, my voice treading the air with caution. "I think this is a mistake. Declan's threats are damning. I get it," I continue, "but it feels like we're missing crucial evidence."

"Detective," Bishop interjects. "We've dug into every corner we could. What more do you suggest?"

"Oh, I don't know—we do our job? Maybe we try to find hard evidence that ties everything together beyond circumstantial allegations!" I snap. "These things take time. Fuck, for all we know, the mayor may have had motive based on the fact that everyone we have met hated this man."

"Watch it, Sanchez," the chief warns.

"I'm sorry, sir, but I'm not ready to close the book on this. Not yet."

The chief's eyes, weary and guarded, meet mine across the weathered expanse of his desk. "Detective," he starts. "I appreciate your tenacity, but we can't ignore the evidence we have. It's compelling, even if only circumstantial. I've made my decision. We're taking what we have to the prosecutor."

"Chief, please." The plea is raw in my throat. "Think about what's at stake. If we're wrong—"

"Detective," he interrupts. "I've made my decision. Is that clear?"

"Sir, I can't sit here and agree when my gut says this is a mistake. Think about it," I persist, ignoring the unspoken warning in his tone. "Declan's alibi hasn't been completely vetted, and those text messages could've been provoked or misconstrued. We need more—"

"Enough!" His fist comes down hard on his desk, a punctuation mark to silence my protest. "Sanchez," the chief continues with a tone cold enough to frost glass, "I didn't want to believe it when Bishop said you seemed distracted, but he's clearly right. As of now, you are off this case. Bishop will take the lead."

My heart hammers against my ribs, betrayal and shock mingling with indignant rage. My head snaps in the direction of my partner, who avoids meeting my gaze. That back-stabbing lazy good-for-nothing . . .

"Chief, you can't—" I say, but he raises his hand again.

"Dismissed, Detective." His voice leaves no room for argument.

Defeated, I push my chair back with a screech against the floor. My gaze lingers on Bishop momentarily before I make my way to the door. As I reach for the handle, I turn back one last time. "This is a mistake," I state firmly as I look at the chief.

Once in the hallway, a whirlwind of thoughts consumes me. The pieces of the puzzle refuse to align in my mind, leaving me with more questions than answers. I can't shake the feeling that something crucial has been overlooked.

A few moments later, I hear Bishop call after me. "Wait, Sanchez." I don't give him the satisfaction of turning around. There's nothing left to say.

I stride down the hallway, and it feels as if the walls

are closing in. All I can think is that I can't be here. I have to be anywhere but inside these four walls. The breeze hits my face when I step outside, clearing the fog of anger and uncertainty. I look up at the steel-gray sky, and all I can think is fuck them. Fuck the chief. Fuck Bishop. Fuck Jason McAllister.

THIRTY-ONE

MARIA

My shoulders sag under the weight of the day. This is the first time in my career I have ever been removed from an investigation. Everything in me told me to stand my ground and argue my point. In everyone's frenzy to close the high-profile case, they are pushing sloppy detective work.

"Mom, what's wrong?" Jordan asks, eyeing me with concern.

I muster a weary smile and brush off the question. "Oh, just a tough day at work, honey. Nothing for you to worry about. How was your first day back to school?"

She shrugs. "It's school—so boring and pointless."

"Glad to see nothing has changed," I say as I pull into our driveway.

"You never told me why you picked me up from school and not Nana Maddie's today. Is she okay?" asks Jordan, always perceptive.

"Nana Maddie is fine, sweetheart. I wanted to spend some time with you tonight," I reply, my mind still swirling with the day's events. As we walk into the house, I see the remnants of a messy living room and a case file scattered on the coffee table.

I ignore the mess and decide to start dinner. Jordan follows me into the kitchen, watching intently as I prepare dinner. She senses when something is bothering me; she always has. I try to shift the conversation away from work, but she doesn't let it go.

"Mom," Jordan says again as she stands near the kitchen island, watching me work. "I can tell something is really bothering you. You can talk to me, you know."

I look into her eyes and see wisdom beyond her years. Jordan has always been perceptive, almost too perceptive for her own good. I take a deep breath and decide that perhaps this is one of the moments in life when I will honestly be a learning example for my daughter.

"Okay, you're right. It was a tough day. My boss basically shut me down on an important case I was working on," I admit, deciding to be honest with my daughter.

"What do you mean shut you down?" she asks, her eyes searching mine.

"As in, I'm off the case."

"What?" Jordan's face reflects a mix of surprise and anger. "But that's not fair!"

I appreciate Jordan's fierce loyalty and protective nature, but I can see the worry in her eyes. She knows how much my work means to me and how invested I get in each case. I stop chopping the vegetables and turn to face her, placing a comforting hand on her shoulder.

"It's okay, Jordan. I'm trying to look at this positively. I've decided to focus on the cases of the victims who don't get all the press coverage and support from the mayor's office," I explain, trying to reassure both her and myself.

Jordan's expression softens as she nods slowly, understanding dawning in her eyes. "That's good. I didn't know things were bad at work. I'm sorry if my skipping school to see Dad added to your stress."

A sense of pride swells within me at her words. Despite my challenges and setbacks at work, knowing I raised a kid like Jordan makes everything worthwhile. I smile at her.

"Thanks, honey. Now, how about you set the table while I finish up here?" I suggest, shifting the focus to a more normal routine for both of us.

As we move around the kitchen, a sense of calm descends. The warmth of our home envelops us like a blanket, shielding us from the harsh realities waiting outside.

Once dinner is in the oven, I move into the living room to tidy up while it cooks. I sweep a strand of hair behind my ear and glance down at the case files strewn across the coffee table. I take the image of the champagne bottle from the McAllister's home. I pause and flip through to the other pictures. One of the glasses appears to have no bubbles in the liquid, while the other one still has what looks like a fair amount.

"Huh," I grunt to myself.

"What is it?" Jordan asks, noticing me pause.

"It just doesn't look right from these crime scene photos. Look at this," I say, pointing at the glass with no bubbles. "This glass was supposedly poured champagne, but there are no bubbles here. Yet the other glass still has some bubbles in it."

Jordan leans in closer, her eyes narrowing as she examines the pictures. "That is strange. Why would there be a difference?"

"I'm not sure," I mumble more to myself than to Jordan. "Maybe this one was poured a considerable amount of time after the other glass."

"Why would that matter?" Jordan asks.

"Because both people who were in the house were supposedly unconscious at the same time. Knocked out by something that had been placed in their drink," I explain, careful not to reveal any of the gruesome details of the case.

"What are you going to do?" she asks.

I sigh, reminded that I am no longer part of the McAllister case. "There's nothing I can do except point out what I noticed when I turn the files in tomorrow."

"Do you think they'll listen to you?"

I don't know the answer to Jordan's question. Today, I was clearly not heard.

"I don't know if they'll listen, but it doesn't mean I won't try," I answer.

As we sit down to dinner, the aroma of a home-cooked meal fills the air. I can't shake off the unease lingering in my mind. The mystery of the champagne glasses plays over and over in my head. But for now, I push it aside.

After dinner, as Jordan settles in for some homework at the kitchen table, I take a moment to review some notes from other cases. The sound of her pencil scratching against paper is oddly comforting.

As much as I try to focus on the work before me, I keep returning to those champagne glasses. Lucas and Victoria both had the Rohypnol in their blood. Could it be that someone else showed up at the house and poured a glass of champagne after the other two were incapacitated? Was it Jason? But if so, why? Or was there someone else there that night, and if so, why would they have poured a fresh glass? Dammit! Nothing about the McAllister case makes sense. As much as I want to be relieved that I am no longer assigned to it, I can't stop my mind from trying to sort out the case.

Glancing at the clock, I realize how much time has passed. With a heavy sigh, I gather the case files. I tuck them away in my bag, determined to bring up my findings to the chief despite no longer officially being on the case. As hurt as I am for not being heard, pursuing the truth will always be my priority.

THIRTY-TWO

MARIA

SIX MONTHS LATER

I step out of my car and look at the house with the For Sale sign in the yard. The last time I was here, crime scene tape surrounded the property, and a dead body was inside. As I walk up to the front door, memories flood back—the flashing lights, the commotion of police officers, and the whispers of neighbors speculating about what happened.

The door is ajar, so I knock softly before pushing it open. Inside, the echo of my entrance collides with cardboard flaps being folded and sealed.

"Victoria?" My voice feels intrusive in the stripped-down space.

She's there, amid a sea of half-filled boxes, with her back to me. As she turns to face me, her eyes widen. "Sanchez, I almost didn't recognize you," she says.

I return the smile and step inside. I take in the boxes scattered around the living room. Victoria is in the process of packing up her life.

"I heard you're leaving," I say, knowing this move is more than a change of address for her.

Victoria nods. "It's time. I can't stay here anymore."

I understand all too well. The ghosts of the past have a way of haunting us, no matter how hard we try to escape them.

"Can I help with anything?" I ask, but she shakes her head, curls bouncing with a defiance that doesn't quite reach her hollowed eyes.

"No, thank you. I need to do this myself." She returns to her task, wrapping a picture frame in newspaper with hands that tremble ever so slightly—if you weren't looking for it, you'd miss it.

"Of course," I murmur, stepping back to give her the semblance of solitude in the thick of upheaval.

"What brings you by today, Detective?" she asks, glancing up at me.

I hesitate, wondering how much I should reveal to the woman who had been a murder suspect of mine not too long ago. I'm no longer a detective for the LA Police Department. In fact, Victoria isn't the only one who will soon enough no longer be a resident of this city.

I take a deep breath, gathering my thoughts before deciding to confide in Victoria about my impending departure from the city. "When I heard you were moving, I wanted to tell you that I'm leaving too," I admit, watching as surprise flickers across her face.

"Leaving? But why?" Victoria is genuinely curious and sets down the picture frame she's packing.

"I suppose I felt like I needed a fresh start. My ex-husband got a job in Oregon, so my daughter and I are going to relocate there as well."

She looks at me as if what I'm saying isn't computing. "You and your ex are getting back together?"

I burst out laughing in response to her question. "Oh God, no! When he told me about the new job, I thought it might be a chance to get out of this city. A fresh start for my daughter and me, and she gets to keep her dad in her life."

Victoria nods solemnly. "You're a good mother."

"Thank you," I say, stepping closer. "My daughter is definitely my entire world."

"I always wondered if Jason would have been a different man if we'd had children." Victoria's confession fills me with sadness for the woman.

I watch Victoria's gaze drift to a photo on the wall, a captured moment frozen in time of her and Jason looking happier than I would have ever imagined them.

"He wasn't the man you thought he was," I state.

Victoria lets out a humorless chuckle. "Seems I have a talent for picking the wrong men," she admits.

"You're not alone in that," I reply, thinking of my own past mistakes.

"If I'm being honest, that wasn't the only reason I wanted to stop by. When I heard about the charges being dropped against Declan Harris, I wanted to check and see how you were doing," I say, watching Victoria for a reaction.

Victoria's eyes widen at the mention of the man's name, a shadow passing over her features. She sets the packing tape down, her hands stilling for a moment before she meets my gaze. "Declan . . ." She trails off as if unsure of what to say.

I can see the turmoil in her expression.

"Do you believe he did it?" I ask quietly.

Victoria's lips part, and a soundless sigh escapes her. "I don't know," she admits at last, her voice barely above a whisper. "I never saw that side of him . . . but then again, I never thought Jason was capable of what he did either."

"I was told about the threatening messages between Declan and Jason," Victoria continues. "But even then . . . I don't know. It's hard to believe someone you cared about could be capable of such things."

"I know, but even good people are capable of terrible acts," I reply. I clear my throat before changing the subject. "I saw the sale of Haven AI still went through."

"Yeah. The board members managed to finalize it even after . . . well, you know," she says before finally glancing at me, a flicker of something unreadable in her eyes. "I try to stay out of the company's affairs. Whatever the board decided to do, that's their business."

"I mean, it's sort of your concern, considering how much money you stand to make from Jason's shares." It was all over the news that Victoria had become one of the wealthiest women in the city after the acquisition, yet she was acting as if it were an insignificant blip on her radar.

She shrugs. "I only want to move on and start

fresh," Victoria replies, her voice tinged with a weariness that speaks of burdens carried far too long. She pauses, turning to face me with a haunted look in her eyes. "Do you ever wonder . . . if things could have been different?"

"Different, how?"

"Like with your husband. If you had made different choices, if you had seen the signs earlier of what was wrong in your marriage?" she asks, and I can see a woman who has been analyzing where her life went off the rails.

"My husband was what was wrong with my marriage. It wouldn't have mattered if I did things differently," I clarify, my words laced with a vulnerability I rarely show.

A flicker of understanding passes between us, a shared recognition of the what-ifs that linger in the corners of our minds.

"Victoria," I say. "Can I ask you something that has been bothering me since I worked on your husband's case?"

Her eyes soften. "Of course."

"I know it was a long time ago, but I noticed in one of the crime scene pictures that the two champagne flutes looked very different. One of the glasses of liquid still had bubbles in it, while the other had none," I explain, my eyes fixed on Victoria as I explain.

"Is there a question in there, Detective?"

I take a deep breath, trying to choose my words carefully. "Do you think that maybe . . . someone else was with Jason that night? Someone who could have been involved in his death?"

Victoria's eyes widen. "Besides Declan?"

I nod. "I can't help but think if it was Declan, we would have found evidence tying him to the scene."

She paces back and forth, her brow furrowed in thought. "But who else could it have been if it wasn't Declan?"

"Do you remember if you or Lucas passed out first?" I inquire.

She halts abruptly and turns to me with a conflicted expression. "Pardon me?"

"That night, do you know which of you passed out first?" I repeat.

She looks away, her hands trembling slightly as she grips the edge of a cardboard box. "I-I can't remember," she stammers.

"It's okay, Victoria. Take your time," I reassure her.

Victoria slowly meets my gaze again. "I . . . I think it was me," she admits. "I remember feeling dizzy, and then everything went black. But when I woke up . . . Jason was already . . ."

"Victoria," I ask, "do you think it's possible that Lucas drank his drink after Jason was already dead?"

"I don't understand what you're asking."

I take a deep breath, trying to find the right way to broach the subject that has been nagging at me since the beginning of this case. "What if . . . Lucas saw you pass out and figured out your drinks had been spiked? What if he was awake when Jason arrived, and they had an altercation?"

Victoria's eyes widen in shock, her hands clenching the edge of the cardboard box tighter. "That's impossible. Lucas would never . . ." she says, her voice faltering.

I place a comforting hand on her shoulder. "I know this is difficult to consider—"

"No!" Victoria exclaims. "One minute, the cops are saying it was Declan, and the next, I'm supposed to believe it was Lucas. The truth is the police have no clue who killed my husband, and I am over the guessing game."

Victoria's outburst echoes through the room.

"I understand. I didn't mean to upset you."

Victoria takes a deep breath. "I just . . . I can't keep living in this constant state of uncertainty. I want closure, Detective. I need to move on from all of this."

Before I leave, I turn to Victoria one last time. "Well, I'll leave you to it. I guess I just wanted to tell you good luck."

"Thank you," she says before walking over to hug me. I'm surprised by the tender gesture. She looks into my eyes and says with a smile, "Let's make a pact. No more toxic relationships for either of us. We can even start a club—The Freedom from Control Freaks Society."

"Sounds exclusive. Do we get membership cards?" I quip, and we both laugh.

"Absolutely." Victoria grins. "And maybe a secret handshake."

"Perfect." I chuckle.

"We're going to need a good one. But for now, let's settle on making sure toxic men regret ever crossing paths with us," Victoria says.

"Deal," I reply.

PART THREE

VICTORIA MCALLISTER

THIRTY-THREE

VICTORIA

The sun beats down, its warmth cradling my body as I lounge under the protective shade of an oversized umbrella. The sand is a canvas of white beneath me, and gentle waves lapping against the shore offer a soothing symphony to my ears. I open one eye just enough to catch the sight of an attractive young man approaching with a grace that seems at odds with the heat. His smile is part of the service here at the Brunei resort, but it's welcomed all the same.

"Your drink, ma'am," he says.

"Thank you," I murmur, accepting the chilled glass filled with a vibrant concoction of tropical flavors and a decorative slice of pineapple perched on the rim. I take a sip, and the cold liquid is a sharp contrast against the day's heat. I allow myself a moment to bask in the beauty of this escape. The resort is nothing short of breathtaking, a luxurious hideaway where recent events feel like distant shadows.

A beautiful blond woman glides toward me. She claims the chaise lounge beside mine with grace.

"I went ahead and ordered you a drink too," I announce.

"Thanks, that's so thoughtful of you," she replies, settling into her seat.

The golden sun flickers across Jenny's features as she smiles and reaches for the drink. "You always know exactly what I need," she says.

"Of course," I murmur. As she sips from the glass, I remember the first time I saw her, not as Jason's assistant but as a woman who had been ensnared by his deceptions just like me.

"How has your morning been?" Jenny asks, tilting her head slightly.

"Oh," I breathed, getting pulled back from the memory. "Very productive," I reply, shifting in my lounge chair to face her more directly. The waves lap at the shore rhythmically. "I met with the real estate agent we found after getting here. We've got several showings lined up."

"Sounds promising," Jenny remarks, the corners of her lips rising in approval.

I take another sip of my tropical drink, feeling the cool liquid slide down my throat, washing away the bitterness. At least for this moment, under the Brunei sun, we can pretend to be just two friends enjoying the serenity of a beachside resort.

"How was your morning?" I arch an eyebrow.

Jenny's gaze drifts past the umbrella's shade, her

expression serene. "Transformative." Her voice is soft. "The massage therapist . . . she had this way of kneading out more than just the knots in my muscles."

I nod. My fingers trace the condensation on my glass, the cool sweat grounding me as I wrestle with the fragments of memory and emotion that threaten to surface.

After a few moments of silence, I say a name I haven't uttered since we stepped off the plane. "Jason," I say, the name a stone dropping into the still waters of our conversation. Jenny's eyes snap back to mine, alert and searching. "It was never going to end well with him, was it?" The question isn't really a question; it's an invitation to unburden.

She shakes her head, golden strands catching the sunlight. "No, but that isn't your fault." Her lips press together.

"Jenny," I say, barely above a whisper, "that night . . ." The images flash before me: the sculpture heavy in my grasp, the shock of impact, Jason's body crumpling to the ground. My heart races, but I steady myself, knowing I'm not alone.

"Victoria, listen to me," Jenny interjects, reaching across the space between our chairs, her hand finding mine. "You did what you had to do. It was self-defense, pure and simple."

"Self-defense . . ." The words echo in my mind. I let out a shuddering breath. "I didn't know it was him that night. I really didn't."

"Shh," Jenny soothes, her thumb rubbing small

circles on the back of my hand. "I know. I know everything." Her blue eyes, clear and resolute, hold mine. "And I stood by you, didn't I? We protected each other."

Protected. The term feels too passive for the violent torrent of that evening—the cold metal of the gun in Jenny's hand, the decisive sound of a single gunshot, and the heavy silence that followed.

The rhythmic lull of the ocean waves creates a soft backdrop to the confessions. I tilt my head back, allowing the sun to kiss my cheeks.

My thoughts drift to Jason and the countless lies. My affair with Declan had begun after I discovered how effortlessly Jason had been lying to me. After testing positive for a sexually transmitted infection, I confronted my husband. He confessed to me that, on occasion, he would visit other women's beds, but that it was only stress relief and didn't mean anything.

The revelation gutted me, but he made it clear he had no intention of changing his behavior. Declan had been my way of seeking revenge for all the pain Jason had caused me. A year after I had been sleeping with Declan, Jason came to me one night, tears in his eyes, begging for forgiveness. He vowed it was all behind us, that he'd never stray again. I feel like such a fool now for believing him. I immediately ended the relationship with Declan, only to have Jenny reach out to me a couple of months later.

"Jason was a master of lies. A serpent with a silver

tongue." The words tumble out of my mouth almost instinctively.

Jenny nods, digesting my words. "That lunch we had," she murmurs, "feels like a lifetime ago now. The one where I told you about . . . me and Jason. About how I didn't know you were still together and he had convinced me there was a future for him and me."

"Jason would never have divorced me," I say. "California's community property laws made sure of that. He knew it too well. He fed you dreams, Jenny. Just like he did with countless others. Fuck, that's what he did to me our entire marriage."

She takes a shaky breath. "I was so humiliated. To think I was the other woman when I thought I was his future. And Jesus, I can't believe I did that to you."

My hand reaches out, brushing hers in a gesture meant to soothe. "And you apologized to me, remember? You didn't need to, but you did."

"Because I felt the weight of it, Victoria. The guilt." Her voice cracks, and she pulls her hand back, wrapping her arms around herself.

"Jenny, we've both been his victims. But that's not who we are anymore." I lock eyes with her, a silent vow passing between us.

That lunch with Jenny was the beginning of a beautiful friendship—one that saved my life. When Jenny overheard that Jason was having me followed, she didn't hesitate to tell me. She went beyond that, though. She told me about the photographs with Lucas. That was how I figured out that Jason thought I was having an affair. She even went as far as going out on a date with Jason's investigator, Marshall.

A chill courses through me, and I reach for my drink, needing something to hold as the memories flood back. The day Jenny called me in a panic because she was out to lunch with Marshall when Jason called and requested Rohypnol. That's when I knew my darling husband was planning something sinister.

I close my eyes, and the night everything changed forever comes flooding back to me. It's like a movie playing in my mind's eye.

The sound of the front door creaking open slices through the silence like a sharp intake of breath. I reach for the closest heavy object I can find. My fingers tighten around the cool marble of the sculpture, a memento from our honeymoon.

That night, I didn't know who to expect. As far as I knew, Jason was in San Francisco, but I had been expecting a visitor of some kind. After all, Jason wouldn't have slipped Rohypnol into my champagne unless he had a reason.

I can see the figure as he takes another step, and my instinct overpowers reason. The sculpture arcs through the air, colliding with an ominous thud against his skull. The man crumples to the floor, unmoving.

"God, what have I done?" Tears blur my vision when I see I have struck Jason.

I don't know how long I sat there with Jason before I called Jenny that night, but she didn't hesitate when I did.

"Jenny . . ." I had choked out between sobs. "He . . . he was going to . . ."

"I know, I know." She pulled me into an embrace. It was the only thing that kept me from shattering into a million pieces that night.

I hadn't even noticed that Jason had a gun in his hand until she pointed it out.

"He wasn't here to talk, Vic," she'd said.

We debated in hushed, urgent whispers. Should we call the police? But deep down, we knew the truth: Jason's influence, his money—nothing would happen to him, and then he would be out and even angrier.

I'm perched on the edge of the chaise lounge now, my fingers tracing the rim of my tropical drink as I take a deep breath. The weight of gratitude is heavy in my chest, and I finally turn to Jenny, her blue eyes holding mine steady.

"Jenny, there's no way I can ever thank you enough for what you did that night." My voice trembles. "Despite everything Jason did, I couldn't pull the trigger." The confession hangs between us, raw and vulnerable.

Jenny reaches out, her hand covering mine with gentle assurance. "Vic, you've got the most loving and forgiving heart of anyone I've ever known. That's why I had to do it—to keep you safe."

I feel a sting of guilt at her words. Jenny doesn't know the whole story. It would devastate her if she did, so she will never know that was always my intention. I didn't know it would end in Jason's death, but I knew when I set my plan into motion that it wouldn't end well for Jason.

All those months ago, when Declan confided in me about the numerous affairs and the way Jason was always complaining about being saddled with me for the rest of his life, I knew. I knew it was time for me to figure a way out of a marriage with that narcissist. I also knew if I were the one who decided I wanted a divorce, he would never let me go. I needed him to want the marriage to end. When I came up with the plan, I had imagined it would result in him divorcing me, but leave it to Jason to decide he was better off with a dead wife rather than an ex-wife.

When Lucas casually mentioned to me at a company event that he was interested in real estate, I saw an opportunity. I would offer to help and then make sure to capture Lucas on our home cameras so that Jason would assume the worst of me, as he always did. I had to practically hit him over the head with the evidence, though, when I messed with the footage on our home cameras. Then when I spotted the man snapping pictures of Lucas and me at lunch, I knew it had to be Jason. That innocent kiss wasn't as innocent as I had made it out to be because I knew in my gut it would push Jason over the edge when he saw the picture.

I didn't set out planning for Jason to meet his end. He did that all by himself. He was the one who took things to the extreme; therefore, I will never feel any guilt for what I did. Jason got exactly what he deserved.

Jenny, though, was innocent in all of this. I used to be innocent—before Jason.

Jenny was the one who shot Jason. She also took care of disposing of the sculpture I used to knock Jason out. When she left me that night, she dropped it off a bridge, never to be seen again.

I swallow hard, remembering how cold the champagne flute felt in my hands after everything was done. I drank the champagne after it was all over. I needed to look like a victim, to maintain the appearance that I had no idea what was happening. When Detective Sanchez mentioned that one of the glasses still had bubbles, I thought perhaps she had figured out what I had done. But instead, it had only made her suspicious of the men around me.

I can tell the detective had been hurt deeply by a man as well. I was so worried she would piece everything together. I think there is some instinctive level of wanting to help other women who have been victimized as well. I believe that is also why Jenny did what she did for me.

"I suppose it's good they dropped the charges against Declan since he was, in fact, innocent," I say, glancing at Jenny.

"Innocent seems like a strong word to use with that man," she replies as she leans forward, her blond hair catching the sunlight like spun gold. "You think he knew what Jason was planning?"

"It wouldn't shock me." The words taste bitter on my tongue. "While we were sleeping together, he told me he knew about all of Jason's affairs." My hands clench involuntarily. "And then when he warned me to stay away from Lucas, I knew he and Jason were openly discussing whether I was having an affair."

"Which means . . ."

"Which means Declan likely knew Jason intended to kill me and did nothing to stop it." The revelation hangs between us, heavy as the tropical air.

We sit in silence for a moment, lost in the gravity of our shared past. Then, as if on cue, we both reach out. Our hands meet halfway across the space that separates our chairs.

"Let's make a pact," I suggest, feeling a newfound resolve coursing through me. "To protect each other from falling into relationships with narcissists."

Jenny's grip tightens, her nails digging slightly into my skin—a physical promise. "No matter the cost," she agrees.

Jenny and I sit side by side, our fingers entwined.

"Victoria," she whispers, "we're in this together, now and always."

I take a deep breath, the scent of the ocean filling my lungs. Our pasts are littered with the wreckage of men like Jason and Declan, who saw us as pawns in their twisted games.

"Here's to new beginnings," I say, lifting my glass in a toast.

"New beginnings," Jenny echoes.

ACKNOWLEDGMENTS

Thank you to the man that adores me in a way I never dreamt was possible. Josh, I don't deserve the deepness of your love, but I'm so happy you disagree. Thank you for supporting my dreams and for pushing me to get the help I needed to learn to be healthy and happy. I wouldn't have this career without you.

Zoe, Brayden, and Penelope, you all make me proud every single day and you have made me a better human. Thank you for being my motivation to get up and keep going every day.

Thank you to Jenny Sims at editing4indies for always jumping into my books when they are at their worst. You make me look smarter than I am. Thank you Karen Lawson for the polish and shine as well as always filling up my cup with your positivity.

To my readers: I wouldn't be able to do what I do without your desire to read my books. Thank you from the bottom of my heart. In addition to readers, thank you to the army of bloggers, ARC readers, and book tokkers that read and review my books. Your time is deeply appreciated and I am honored you have taken your time to read and review my work.

ABOUT THE AUTHOR

Wendy Owens writes the kind of "what if?" questions that keep you up past your bedtime. What if your husband's new fiancée visited you in prison? What if your father's crimes came looking for you twenty years later? What if the person you trusted most was the one you should have feared?

An Ohio native, Wendy is the author of more than twenty-five books spanning psychological thrillers, dark romance, cozy mysteries, and fantasy — stories that live in very different worlds but always come down to the same thing: relationships, impossible choices, and consequences that feel earned.

When she isn't writing, Wendy is usually with her family and her dogs, planning her next trip, or reading. Preferably all three.

Start with My Husband's Fiancée to see what her readers won't shut up about.

To follow everything current with Wendy Owens' Books:
https://signup.wendyowensbooks.com/

ALSO BY WENDY OWENS

Find links to all of Wendy's Books at wendyowensbooks. com/books/

PSYCHOLOGICAL THRILLER

My Husband's Fiancée (book1)

My Wife's Secrets (book 2)

The Day We Died

An Influential Murder

Secrets At Meadow Lake

An Affair to Die For

Couple Seeking Boyfriend (Spicy)

Couple Seeking Girlfriend (Spicy)

SPICY DARK MAFIA ROMANCE

Crimson Ties

Crimson Fate

Crimson Vows

Crimson Sins

COZY MYSTERIES

Jack Be Nimble, Jack Be Dead

O Deadly Night

Roses Are Red, Violet is Dead

YA

Wash Me Away

CONTEMPORARY ROMANCE (adult)

Stubborn Love

Only In Dreams

The Luckiest

Do Anything

It Matters to Me

URBAN FANTASY

Burning Destiny

Blazing Moon

Blood Spark

YA PARANORMAL (clean)

Sacred Bloodlines

Unhallowed Curse

The Shield Prophecy

The Lost Years

The Guardians Crown

---

www.ingramcontent.com/pod-product-compliance
Lightning Source LLC
La Vergne TN
LVHW040216110826
845146LV00005B/1312

* 9 7 9 8 9 9 1 6 2 2 7 5 2 *